Puffin Books

MR BROWSER AND THE SPACE MAGGOTS

There's a weird atmosphere at Chivvy Chase School. The children are feeling restless and it rains every playtime yet the field is turning brown. Selwyn, Anna and Spiky decide to visit the new warden at the local Nature Reserve in Chivvy Chase woods to find out why. But when they get there the warden has strangely disappeared leaving messages about Space Maggots and bubbles from the sky. From that moment the children realize something is wrong.

Together with Mr Browser they go on dawn patrol in the woods, looking for cloud capsules and space maggots. But when Spiky runs off on his own he discovers an evil plot to poison not only Chivvy Chase School but the whole world!

Spiky's desperate attempt to stop this extraterrestrial invasion makes an exciting and often hilarious read. This is a highly topical story and a marvellous follow-up to Philip Curtis's other Mr Browser adventures.

D0416121

Other books by Philip Curtis

MR BROWSER AND THE BRAIN SHARPENERS
MR BROWSER AND THE COMET CRISIS

Philip Curtis

Mr Browser and
the Space Maggots

Illustrated by Tony Ross

PUFFIN BOOKS

PUFFIN BOOKS

Published by the Penguin Group
27 Wrights Lane, London W8 5TZ, England
Viking Penguin Inc., 40 West 23rd Street, New York, New York 10010, USA
Penguin Books Australia Ltd, Ringwood, Victoria, Australia
Penguin Books Canada Ltd, 2801 John Street, Markham, Ontario, Canada L3R 1B4
Penguin Books (NZ) Ltd, 182–190 Wairau Road, Auckland 10, New Zealand

Penguin Books Ltd, Registered Offices: Hardmondsworth, Middlesex, England

First published by Andersen Press Limited 1989
Published in Puffin Books 1990
10 9 8 7 6 5 4 3 2 1

Text copyright © Philip Curtis, 1989
Illustrations copyright © Tony Ross, 1989
All rights reserved

Filmset in Baskerville

Made and printed in Great Britain by
Richard Clay Ltd, Bungay, Suffolk

Contents

1   It Always Rains at Playtimes

'What's the time, Spiky?' whispered Michael Fairlie, putting up the lid of his desk to hide the sound of his voice from Mr Browser as he spoke. Spiky looked at his digital watch, which told him that it was the month of May and that the time was 10.15 a.m. on Thursday the 15th.

'Quarter past ten,' whispered Spiky.

'Quarter past ten and a blue sky,' said Michael. 'Looks as though we might be able to go out to play for once. Do you realize, Spiky, that every day so far this week we've had to stay in at playtime because it's been raining!'

'Of course I do,' replied Spiky. 'Our playground football match against Class 7 has been postponed for ages now, but we'll start today.'

'But Mark's away,' said Michael.

'I'll play,' put in Anna Cardwell from behind them.

'You!' was Spiky's comment.

'She's quite good,' said Michael.

'And I might as well play, because the football game breaks up most of the other games in the whole playground,' grumbled Anna. 'You can't even skip without the rope being pulled out of your hand by mad hordes of boys.'

'Quiet!' ordered Mr Browser, looking up from his desk. 'You've only about ten minutes left to finish your work, and if you don't do so I might keep you in at playtime even if it is fine!'

Class 8 became quiet, because even those like Selwyn Jordan, who were not so keen on playground games, were looking forward to a break in the fresh air for a change. Mr Browser himself was secretly keeping an eye on the weather, because he, too, was hoping the children could all go outside at playtime instead of being kept in the school, which meant that he couldn't enjoy his cup of tea at all peacefully. That was why he had said 'I might keep you in' because he knew very well that even if Spiky Jackson had performed a dance on his desk, he would have found a different punishment for him than keeping him in school that playtime.

But Spiky and all the rest were quiet, waiting hopefully for the bell to be rung. Miss Copewell, the secretary, pressed a button in her office, and it acted like magic on Class 8 and their teacher.

'Playtime – and it's fine,' said Anna, shutting her book sharply. Mr Browser was as prompt.

'All stand,' he said. 'I want everyone outside at once. We must make the best of the fine weather.'

'It's beginning to cloud over,' Selwyn pointed out, but no one took any notice of him.

'Lead on!' ordered Mr Browser, and in ten seconds the classroom was empty of children.

Mr Browser tidied his desk and set off on the way to the Staffroom – but to his annoyance he was interrupted before he could reach it.

'Oh, George, please fetch your tea and come into my room for a moment, will you. I've something to discuss with you.' Mr Sage, the Headmaster, was standing at his door waiting for Mr Browser to pass.

'Of course, Mr Sage,' said Mr Browser, and fetched his tea, not without grumbling that on this, the first outdoor playtime for a long while, he couldn't enjoy his cup of tea in peace.

He sat down on the visitor's chair in Mr Sage's room and waited to be told why he was there. Miss Copewell came in with a cup of tea for the Headmaster. Somebody in Class 8 must have been up to something, thought Mr Browser, but he kept quiet, because it's unwise to anticipate trouble. Mr Sage put a pill in his tea and took a small sip.

'Miss Copewell and I have just been saying,' he began, 'that the school has become rather noisy of late.'

Mr Browser stirred his tea.

'Yes, and there have been lots of squabbles and fights lately,' put in Miss Copewell. 'Even the girls have started pulling one another's hair and jumping on one another's toes.'

'It's not like Chivvy Chase School,' observed Mr Sage, and seeing Mr Browser's raised eyebrows he quickly went on: 'I mean it's unusual for these things to be happening so often. We've always had a good spirit here.'

'Perhaps it's the fault of the bad weather,' suggested Mr Browser, hoping that his class was not going to be specially mentioned. 'They've been penned in every day this week.'

'Maybe,' agreed the Headmaster. 'But something must be done, and I thought that as your class is at the top of the school, the example should come from there.'

'What do you want me to do?' asked Mr Browser, but before Mr Sage could reply the conversation was interrupted by Mr Caracco, who put his head round the door.

'It's raining again,' he announced. 'Looks nasty, too. Shall I bring them inside?'

'Oh – bother!' said Mr Sage. 'Yes, you'd better, I suppose. Ring the bell, Miss Copewell, please. They'll have to spend the rest of playtime in their classrooms. Make sure the teachers return promptly to their rooms, Mr Browser. It's at times like these that trouble can occur.'

'It's uncanny,' observed Mr Browser, 'how it always rains at playtimes. No wonder the children are restless.'

'That's no excuse,' said Mr Sage irritably, and Mr Browser took his tea back to the Staffroom and warned his colleagues that Mr Sage, as he always put it, was on the rampage.

'He's looking for trouble,' he added, and the teachers downed their tea and returned to their rooms.

Out in the playground Selwyn Jordan couldn't help smiling when others began complaining about the rain.

'I told you it was clouding over,' he said to Spiky. 'I knew the rain was coming.'

'Just when we were winning,' complained Spiky. 'Why does the weather always choose playtimes? And it's such rotten rain, too. It has a funny taste about it.'

'It's not meant for drinking,' said Anna as they led back into school.

'He's right, though,' said Selwyn, holding out his hand in the rain and then licking it. 'It tastes acidy. Mr Springfield says that's caused by pollution.'

'What's pollution?' asked Anna.

'Pollution is when they let sewers flow into the sea,' said Spiky.

'It's caused by all sorts of things,' Selwyn tried to explain. 'The countryside is being slowly poisoned, he says. He's always going on about it.'

'Who is Mr Springfield, anyway?' demanded Spiky. 'What does he know about it?'

'He's the new Warden of the Nature Reserve in Chivvy Chase woods,' said Selwyn. 'He's come to live as a lodger with us. He says the Nature Reserve is in trouble from pollution. The trees are dying off, and the grass is becoming brown, and the squirrels and birds are suffering.'

'Our school field is turning brown too,' said Anna. 'Maybe he's right.'

'It's a lot of fuss about nothing,' declared Michael Fairlie. 'Things always dry up in the summer.'

'But not in May,' remarked Selwyn.

'You think he's right, don't you!' said Spiky.

'I don't know,' replied Selwyn. 'But he's a very nice man, and he's getting terribly worried about it. He's clever, too. He can show you all kinds of creatures in the woods – and plants. I've been to his lodge with my mother. He said that he'd be pleased to see any of us if we wanted to visit him, and he'd show us where foxes and rabbits and a badger live.'

'They don't live all together, do they, Selwyn?' joked Anna, and Selwyn ignored her.

'I'll come with you, Selwyn,' said Spiky, always ready to strike while the iron was hot. 'It's not far to the woods. We could go there after school.'

'I'll come too,' said Anna. Selwyn looked a little disturbed.

'I'll have to let my mother know first,' he said.

'We'll go past your house on the way,' suggested Spiky, not to be put off, and Selwyn agreed.

The rain washed against the windows of Class 8's room, and soon all conversation had to stop because Miss Copewell rang the bell for the end of playtime. Irritably Mr Browser called for them to take out their geography notebooks, and irritably they obeyed, with much clatter and noise.

'Things are growing worse in this school,' thought Mr Browser. 'I really don't know why I became a teacher.'

Downstairs in his study Mr Sage dealt irritably with several children who had been sent to him by irritated teachers, and ended by standing over one luckless boy and scaring him more than he had Spiky when Spiky threw Anna Cardwell into the swimming pool in the previous summer.

'I don't know what's come over me,' thought Mr Sage afterwards. 'I must be growing old and irritable. The poor lad hadn't done anything seriously wrong at all.'

In the Staffroom, Miss Copewell irritably washed

up the cups and saucers – and dropped a cup on the floor.

'This shouldn't be my job,' she thought. 'I wish I were a secretary in a bank, or somewhere else more peaceful than this.'

And the cloud passed on, and slight irritation spread over the whole Chivvy Chase area. Car drivers shook their fists at one another, shopkeepers grumbled at their assistants, and customers became irritated with the shopkeepers. In hundreds of homes people irritably performed their household duties – spilling milk and breaking crockery and grumbling most of the time.

Gradually the day ground on its irritating way at Chivvy Chase School, until at half past three teachers and children closed their books with sighs of relief as Miss Copewell rang the bell for the end of school.

'Let's get away to the Nature Reserve as soon as we can,' said Spiky to Selwyn. 'I'm dying for some fresh air.'

'I hope my mother lets us go,' replied Selwyn, and Spiky pulled a face. He seldom stopped to ask his mum's permission to go anywhere, partly because very often she wasn't there to ask – but he knew that Selwyn's position was different, as after Selwyn's father died his mother began to fuss over him much more.

They ran most of the way to Selwyn's house, and Spiky and Anna stayed outside kicking their heels while Selwyn sought permission. Mrs Jordan was only just recovering from an irritating day – she had broken a cup belonging to her best coffee set – and she was doubtful mostly about the presence of Spiky on the proposed visit. But she felt like having a rest after her trying day.

'It's a fine afternoon, so you can go,' she agreed. 'But make sure that Simon doesn't get you into any mischief. Straight there and straight back afterwards, remember – and tell Mr Springfield that I'll have a steak and kidney pie ready for him at seven o'clock. Here you are – take this bar of chocolate and share it with Simon and Anna to keep you going until you come home.'

The bar of chocolate was a large one, so Anna and Spiky were both well pleased that they had decided to visit the Nature Reserve as they munched their portions and hurried along the road to the Chivvy Chase woods. It was easy for Spiky to imagine the woods as a jungle taking over from civilization. The streets and houses of the town first gave way to playing fields and a golf course, riding stables and a bowling green. The holes of the golf course were separated by areas of woodland which ran out like fingers from the main woods.

They followed a path along one of these outrunners, and after a while the golf course was left behind and the trees closed in around them. Yet further on they came to a gate set in an iron fence – and beyond the gate was the wildest part of the woods, the Nature Reserve. They pushed the gate open, crossed a small bridge over a stream which was little more than a ditch, and entered what Spiky termed the heart of the jungle. He had been there once with a school party, some years back, when the previous Warden had given a talk about the wild creatures which were supposed to live in the Reserve; he had shown them rabbit holes, fox holes and birds' nests – but none of the creatures had obliged by making an appearance, which made the lecture rather boring. Since then he had visited the Reserve only to collect conkers, climb trees and play various kinds of hide-and-seek games. These became almost too exciting at times, because the Reserve was large enough for children to lose themselves in it easily.

For once Selwyn was able to act as leader, for he had visited the place more often, and knew the route to the wooden hut where the Warden had a kind of woodland classroom, complete with a blackboard and wooden benches and tables. On the walls were maps and pictures of birds and animals, together with lists of all the different kinds of plants and wild flowers to be found in the woods.

'It's not as nice as it used to be here,' said Anna, as she and Spiky trotted after Selwyn. 'Some of the trees are dead, and the grass is brown at the ends of the blades, like the grass on our school field.'

'That's caused by pollution,' explained Selwyn. 'Mr Springfield used to talk about it often.'

'Used to?' queried Spiky.

'He doesn't talk about it now,' went on Selwyn. 'I think he must have given up hope of trying to stop it.

He'll tell us about it if you want to know more. Turn right where the paths next cross, and we'll be there.'

'I hope he's in,' said Anna.

'He'll be there – or not far away,' said Selwyn confidently. 'Mostly he goes out and about in the early morning, and before he locks up in the evening he writes up his reports and letters. If he has gone out, he'll not be far away. Turn right here.'

They turned right – and about a hundred metres ahead of them they could see the wooden hut, which was surrounded by a wire fence, almost as though it was feared that wild animals might attack the Warden. In reality it was human vandals that the local council worried about. The gate was open, and Selwyn went to the door of the hut and knocked. There was no reply.

'It looks to me as if the door's open,' said Spiky, and without waiting for the more polite Selwyn, he pushed against it.

The door creaked open, and they stared inside. It was a gloomy room, because the windows were small and the trees all around kept out much light – but they could see at once that all was not well.

'Mr Springfield!' called out Selwyn. 'We thought we'd like to come and see you – '

'He's not there!' Spiky interrupted him. 'Something's wrong here – all his papers on the floor, and his desk half pushed off its platform.'

'Perhaps he's in the little room at the back,' persisted

Selwyn, not liking to think that he had brought them all the way for nothing.

'The place smells funny!' remarked Anna as Selwyn pulled open the door to the tiny cloakroom at the back.

'No one there!' admitted Selwyn.

'If you ask me he's left very suddenly – perhaps he's been attacked,' declared Spiky.

'Who would attack a Nature Reserve Warden?' asked Selwyn – but the state of the room forced him to admit to himself that something could be wrong.

'Let's pick up his papers,' suggested Anna. 'Maybe he'll come back while we're doing it.'

This was said chiefly to try and ease Selwyn's mind, for he was looking very worried. Most of the papers on the floor were leaflets of various kinds, some about plants and trees, and one or two about pollution.

'What's this?' asked Spiky, picking up a torn piece of notepaper. 'Somebody's scribbled something on it.'

He held up the paper near a window, and the other two stood beside him, screwing up their eyes to read the hurried words scrawled on the paper.

'Beware of the bubbles from the sky!' ran the message. 'My fears have come true – the Space Maggots are here! Read my letter, and believe it. I'm under attack and I may not come – '

At this point the scrawl stopped.

'Bubbles from the sky? Space Maggots?' said Spiky. 'Has he gone mad?'

'He's always been very sensible,' said Selwyn. 'Something strange must have happened!'

'Let's try and find the letter he mentioned,' said Anna. 'Perhaps that will explain everything.'

But hard as they searched, they could find no letter anywhere in the building. The strange smell in the place made them more and more uneasy, and soon they were glad to open the door and go out into the fresh air.

The woods were still and silent, and as they started for home even the noise of their own footsteps able to alarm them.

2 Selwyn Finds a Letter

Only when they reached the first houses along the road which ran level with the woods did they relax and slow down. Selwyn was the first to speak.

'I think we ought to tell the police,' he said. 'I'm sure Mr Springfield wouldn't leave the door open and the room in such a mess. He's always been such a tidy man.'

'Has he any enemies?' asked Spiky.

'Not that I know of. He's very friendly, and keeps himself to himself, my mother says. He often talks to me about school and what Mr Browser teaches us – specially about Nature study.'

'Has he said anything to you about the woods lately?' asked Anna. 'I mean anything unusual – '

'Not really,' said Selwyn, and then he frowned. 'He has been a bit upset in the last weeks – my mother said he must be overworking. Sometimes he went out very early indeed in the morning, but he said it was in order to see the animals when everything was quiet. He was rather sad at times, because he said the plants and grass in the woods were slowly dying. I remember one day he told my mother, "The grass is doomed, and so are we," and she told him to cheer up and gave him something to drink.'

'What do you think he meant by that?' asked Spiky.

'Something to do with pollution, I think. That means the gradual killing of plant life by the chemicals we use. He often said the air isn't pure any more – even the rain is dirty.'

'And it's rained an awful lot lately,' said Spiky.

'And often around playtimes,' added Anna. 'Perhaps your mother can tell us more about him, Selwyn.'

They hurried to Selwyn's house, where his mother came to the door to greet them.

'About time you were back.' she said. 'Is Mr Springfield on his way? I've cooked a steak and kidney pie for him, and I don't want it to dry up.'

'Mr Springfield wasn't there,' Selwyn told her.

'Not there? He must have left early. Perhaps he's shopping in the town.'

'He hadn't locked up. The door was open, and his table had been tipped over. All his papers were lying on the floor.'

Mrs Jordan stared at her son, and at the earnest faces of Spiky and Anna.

'Oh dear,' she said. 'Poor Mr Springfield.'

'Do you think he's been attacked?' asked Anna.

'Attacked?' repeated Mrs Jordan looking puzzled. 'Attacked – no, my dear. But he's been acting rather oddly lately. I really think we ought to contact the police. Are you quite sure that he wasn't anywhere about?'

'Quite sure,' said Selwyn, and Spiky nodded agreement. It was clear that, even if Mrs Jordan didn't think Mr Springfield had been attacked, she was afraid that something unpleasant could have happened to him.

'I'm going to phone the police,' she said suddenly.

'May we go now?' asked Anna, thinking of her favourite television programme.

'Not yet, please,' replied Mrs Jordan. 'You'd all better wait here until I know what the police are going to do.'

They waited patiently while she made the call and told someone at the police station of her fears for Mr Springfield.

'You have to stay here until the police come,' she told them when the phone conversation ended. 'They want to ask you some questions.'

They had to wait about a quarter of an hour before a police car drew up outside the house. A plain clothes police officer stepped out of it, looking very serious. Selwyn's mother, who had turned pale at the sight of a police car standing outside her house, opened the door quickly and let him inside.

'Sorry to have kept you,' he said, 'but we sent two men to the Nature Reserve, and they have just reported that the scene there is just as the children described. I take it that these are the children?'

He turned to the three children and stared at them them with a piercing look in his eyes, far worse than that of a teacher who suspects somebody has been up to something.

'Are you quite sure it was like that when you first entered the hut?' he demanded. Spiky was the first to realize what the detective had in mind.

'You don't think we wrecked the place, do you?' he replied, while Anna and Selwyn stared in bewilderment. 'Would we have told about it if we had?'

'Of course we didn't,' put in Anna, finding her voice.

'Mr Springfield lives here,' said Selwyn. 'I wouldn't do that to him.'

Their earnestness seemed to convince the detective.

'I'm inclined to believe you,' he said looking a little less stern. 'I have to ask questions like that – after all, I've never met you before.'

'Are your men still looking for Mr Springfield?' asked Selwyn.

'We're making a limited search, but he may well have gone off somewhere before the hut was broken into, so we have to hope that he'll turn up safe and well.'

'He wrote a message,' said Spiky, putting his hand in his pocket and bringing out a crumpled piece of paper. 'At least we think he must have written it.' He handed over the paper. The detective opened it out and read it raising his eyebrows as he did so.

'Bubbles from the sky? Space Maggots?' He shook his head. 'This doesn't make much sense. Where is the letter he mentions?'

'I don't know,' Selwyn told him. 'We couldn't find a letter.'

'I don't know anything about a letter,' added Mrs Jordan as the detective looked at her.

'He was worrying about pollution,' said Selwyn.

'Pollution. Hmm.' The detective looked at Mrs
Jordan and again shook his head. He was about to ask
her a question when he appeared to remember that
the children were standing there.

'You two had better get off home,' he said. 'I'd like
to take your names and addresses first, in case I need
to come and talk to your parents.'

'My mum and dad don't know anything about it,'
declared Anna.

'He means he can't ask you questions unless they're

with you,' explained Spiky – and the detective gave him a sharp look.

'Off you go now,' he said, 'and I don't suppose you'll hear anything more from me. I expect Mr Springfield will turn up in due course.'

When Anna and Spiky had gone, he turned to Mrs Jordan. 'I'd like to have a word with you alone, please,' he said.

'Go into the kitchen, Selwyn,' said his mother. 'You'll find something there for you to eat.'

'Before you go, Selwyn,' said the detective suddenly, 'have you noticed anything unusual about Mr Springfield lately?'

'Not really,' replied Selwyn. 'He's been quite interested in my school – wanted to know how the children were behaving and whether the teachers were more bad-tempered than usual. And he asked about the grass – '

'The grass?' The detective was surprised.

'Yes, he wanted to know if the grass on the school field was growing properly – and of course, it isn't. It's more brown than green this year.'

'I'm sure this gentleman doesn't want to know about the school grass, Selwyn,' put in Mrs Jordan.

'Well, he asked me,' replied Selwyn. 'I suppose Mr Springfield was thinking about pollution.'

'Thank you, Selwyn,' said the detective. 'Anything else?'

'No, nothing,' said Selwyn with a touch of sulkiness.

'All right, Mrs Jordan. I'll have to ask if I can take

a look at Mr Springfield's room, just to see that everything's in order there.'

'Surely he doesn't suspect my mum!' thought Selwyn, and stood there wondering if he should be around to protect her.

'Off you go, Selwyn!' she told him, and he made for the kitchen as they moved to the foot of the stairs.

Once inside the kitchen, he waited until he heard their footsteps reach the top of the stairs, then came out into the hall. As soon as they had entered Mr Springfield's room he crept up the stairs and into his own bedroom. There he left the door ajar and did his best to listen to the conversation.

'He's a very tidy man,' Mrs Jordan was saying. 'Very serious – he takes his work so to heart. He hates it when he finds people have ill treated animals or interfered with birds' nests. I keep telling him people aren't perfect, but he seems to expect them to be.'

'To tell you the truth, Mrs Jordan,' came the voice of the detective, 'this looks to me as if it could be some kind of nervous breakdown. Writing about Space Maggots and bubbles in the air – well, you wouldn't expect that from a normal person, especially one like Mr Springfield, if your description of him is right.'

'Oh dear, oh dear,' said Mrs Jordan. 'I do hope he hasn't done himself any harm. His room looks the same as ever, I must say.'

'Good,' said the detective. 'Then we'll hope for the best. Until he reappears, would you please leave his room as it is?'

'Of course I will. I'll lock the door now,' said Mrs Jordan – and Selwyn heard her do this as they came out on the landing.

'Poor Mr Springfield!' his mother was saying again as they went downstairs. While she was busy seeing the detective out, Selwyn took the chance to slip downstairs and begin his meal in the kitchen, a meal for which he had little appetite.

When his mother came and joined him she looked pale and upset, and fussed around with crockery and pots and pans just to give herself something to do. The table was laid for Mr Springfield's meal, and she kept on looking at the empty place.

'Whatever can have happened to him?' she muttered once or twice, more to herself than to Selwyn, who finally removed himself from her nervous wonderings and switched on the television. But he found it difficult to lose himself in any of the programmes. His mind, like his mother's, was intent on trying to puzzle out what had happened to Mr Springfield. Had he been attacked, or had a brainstorm, or simply gone away because he was tired of his work?

'He's not coming back tonight, it seems,' said Mrs Jordan, joining Selwyn. 'I've put his meal away – '

The ringing of the telephone interrupted her, surprising them both.

'Perhaps it's Mr Springfield,' said Mrs Jordan, and hurried to the hall to pick up the phone.

'No, he's not come back,' Selwyn heard her say. 'Yes, of course I'll let you know as soon as he does – if he does.'

'It wasn't him,' she told Selwyn. 'It was the police. They haven't found him, and they want me to let them know as soon as he comes back.'

They sat silently watching television for some time, until it was nearly nine o'clock.

'You'd better go to bed now, Selwyn,' said his mother. 'I shan't be late myself – all this excitement has made me tired.'

'It's a bit early, Mum,' protested Selwyn half-heartedly. In secret, he was pleased to go up to the quiet of his bedroom where he could think about the day's events without being disturbed. He sat on his bed for a while, and even took out a book and tried to read, but found he couldn't concentrate. He put the book away and undressed. Leaving the bedside light on, he climbed into bed and lay looking up at the ceiling.

He was about to switch the light off, but first of all shifted his pillow to place it in a more comfortable position. As he moved it a slight crackling sound came from underneath it. Curious, he pulled the pillow away. Lying underneath it was an envelope. Selwyn picked it up and held it underneath his bedside lamp to read the address on it.

'URGENT' was written in capital letters at the top right hand corner and beneath it were the words: 'To Mr Browser, Selwyn's teacher.'

Selwyn stared at the envelope as if it were a snake, ready to spring at him. The writing was undoubtedly Mr Springfield's. What could he have wanted to write to Mr Browser about? Could this be a secret report on

Selwyn himself? Sometimes Mr Springfield did seem to think that he could try and take the place of Selwyn's father. Or was it the letter which was mentioned in the note which Spiky had picked up in the hut? Mr Springfield had no reason to complain about Selwyn, as far as he knew. But why should a letter about anything else be addressed to Mr Browser? Why should he write to Mr Browser about something which may have happened in the woods? Selwyn lay back and held the letter up in front of him, wishing that he could read its contents.

He was first inclined to take it downstairs and show it to his mother, but quickly decided against this. Clearly, if Mr Springfield had wanted Mrs Jordan to know about it, he would have addressed the letter to her. Should the police be told about it? Maybe it was just a personal note to Mr Browser about a possible class trip to the Nature Reserve. If not, then Mr Browser himself could inform the police. The letter was sealed and addressed to Mr Browser, and Selwyn was the kind of boy who wouldn't wish to deceive anyone. Opening it would be to deceive Mr Browser and betray Mr Springfield. So he tucked the envelope under his pillow and switched off the light.

He pretended to be asleep when his mother came upstairs to bed an hour later, but it was nearly midnight before he fell into an uneasy sleep which was disturbed all night long by strange dreams.

3   The Hole in the Sky

When Selwyn awoke in the morning he stared up at the ceiling, aware that although everything looked normal, something was to be unusual about the day. Then he remembered the letter, and hastily felt underneath his pillow. Yes, it was still there! Swiftly he jumped out of bed and put it in one of his trouser pockets. He was already dressing when his mother called out to him that he should get up.

He came down to breakfast and had to listen to warnings, grumblings and words of regret from his mother.

'On no account must you go into poor Mr Springfield's room, Selwyn,' she told him. 'He hasn't come home yet, and I've been lying awake for most of the night hoping to hear him come in. The police will probably come back again, though what they can find to help them I'm sure I don't know. It's not as if we ever had any trouble with him. Oh dear – how curious the neighbours are going to be if they see policemen coming in and out of the house! Don't go telling anyone at school about what has happened, will you!'

'But they're sure to know. Anna and Spiky are

bound to have told almost everybody,' Selwyn reminded her.

'Get on with your breakfast,' said his mother, annoyed by the realization that what Selwyn had said was true. 'Poor Mr Springfield! Wherever can he be? I do hope he hasn't come to any harm.'

Selwyn gobbled up his breakfast, anxious to escape from his mother's nervous chatter. The letter crackled now and again when he put his hand in his pocket to make sure it was still there. Swallowing a last gulp of tea, he escaped to school, glad that he hadn't bothered his mother with the letter. Deep inside him, Selwyn knew that since his father had died his mother had taken to worrying too much about everything; he couldn't stop her doing so, but at least he could keep unnecessary worries out of her way.

He was one of the first to arrive at school, and he dawdled about on the path from which he could most easily see the car-park, an area which was forbidden to children. When he arrived, Mr Browser would have to come across to the path in order to enter school.

'What's keeping you, Selwyn?' asked Michael Fairlie as he ran past.

'I'm waiting for Spiky,' replied Selwyn, to satisfy him. In fact, Spiky was not long in coming.

'What's happened, Selwyn?' he asked. 'Did the police tell your mum what it was all about?'

'I don't think they know themselves,' replied Selwyn. 'They've locked his room and they may be

33

coming back, that's all I know. He hasn't come home yet.'

Spiky gave Selwyn a knowing look.

'Coming back if they find out it's murder?' he suggested, but Selwyn shook his head.

'They didn't say that,' he assured Spiky.

'What are you hanging about here for?'

'I – I want to see Mr Browser,' admitted Selwyn.

'Well, you're in luck. I can see him coming now.'

Mr Browser's old car chugged into the car-park, and Selwyn wished that Spiky would go away – but he didn't stir. Mr Browser took out his briefcase, which was so full of books that he couldn't close it properly, locked his car and came towards the path, seeming not to be in a hurry to be at school. Spiky stood there, waiting for Selwyn to give his message. With Mr Browser almost upon him, Selwyn couldn't delay longer.

'What do you boys want?' asked Mr Browser, who was not in the best of moods because he was on playground duty that day and so would have little time to himself.

'Please, Mr Browser, I've a letter for you,' said Selwyn, suddenly bringing the letter out of his pocket, to the surprise of Spiky. 'It's from the Nature Reserve Warden, Mr Springfield,' he added.

'Ah, yes,' said Mr Browser, taking the letter. 'No doubt he wants me to fix up a class visit.'

'Mr Springfield has vanished!' announced Spiky.

'I beg your pardon?' said Mr Browser, looking at the envelope.

'He's vanished, Mr Browser. Anna and Selwyn and I went to his hut in the woods, and he wasn't there, and it was all turned upside down, and the police called at Selwyn's and they're still out searching for him – '

'Is this true, Selwyn?' asked Mr Browser, looking doubtfully from the letter to Spiky.

'Yes, Mr Browser. It's all true. He must have written the letter before he went to work yesterday. I found it under my pillow last night.'

Other children were coming past them along the path, and Mr Browser didn't wish to discuss such a strange affair in front of them.

'All right, Selwyn,' he said. 'I'll speak to you later. Thank you for the letter. Now you'd better be off to the playground.'

They obeyed, but as soon as they reached the playground Spiky rounded on Selwyn.

'What's this letter all about?' he demanded.

'How should I know?' replied Selwyn. 'It was addressed to Mr Browser.'

'But it was written in your house. You could have opened it,' blustered Spiky, annoyed.

'Of course I couldn't,' insisted Selwyn. 'Do you open letters addressed to other people?'

'Then you should have given it to the police,' said Spiky grumpily. 'Why should he write to Browser?'

'Don't ask me,' declared Selwyn. 'Maybe it was to do with a visit, like Mr Browser said.'

'I bet it wasn't,' said Spiky, and then the conversation ceased, because they were joined by Anna and some of her friends. Clearly Anna had recovered from her fright in the woods, and was enjoying telling them all about the affair.

'Selwyn!' she called out. 'Did the police let you come to school?'

'Of course they did.'

'He's had a letter,' put in Spiky. 'A letter addressed to Mr Browser.'

'What's in it?' asked Anna at once.

'I'd give anything to know,' Spiky declared, and Selwyn turned away from the group, disturbed and wondering whether he ought to have handed the letter over to the police after all.

Shortly afterwards Mr Browser appeared in the playground, whistle in hand, now and then looking at his watch.

'Why don't you ask him what's in the letter?' persisted Anna, pulling at Selwyn's arm.

'I can't – it's his letter, not mine,' replied Selwyn irritably.

'Then I shall,' declared Anna, and ran straight up to Mr Browser. 'Please, Mr Browser, was the letter Selwyn brought you about what happened to Mr Springfield?'

'It was a private letter, Anna,' replied Mr Browser, giving her one of his looks of displeasure.

'I know – but does it say why he's disappeared, Mr Browser?'

'No, Anna,' said Mr Browser, frowning. 'I must blow the whistle now.'

He did, and all talking stopped. Then Mr Browser

made a big mistake. Usually he kept his own class back until last, but perhaps because he was faced with curious looks from Spiky, Anna and Selwyn, he decided to let Class 8 into school first.

'Class 8, lead in – and I hope I can trust you to settle down sensibly until I come in myself.'

Class 8 led on, many of them not particularly pleased to have the privilege of leading into school first. On arriving in the classroom most of them went to their seats, but Anna Cardwell stood by Mr Browser's table, on which his now empty briefcase was standing, with a pile of marked books next to it.

'Spiky! Selwyn!' Anna spoke in one of those stage whispers which will carry further than ordinary talking. 'Come here!'

Spiky and Selwyn joined her, and she pointed to an envelope lying in front of the briefcase. The letter it contained was half in the envelope and half out, as though Mr Browser had been reading it and then suddenly realized that he ought to be on duty in the playground, and had hastily tucked it back in the envelope.

'That's the letter!' said Anna. 'Selwyn, I'm right aren't I?'

'Yes,' said Selwyn. 'But – '

'I'm going to read it,' said Anna.

'You can't,' said Selwyn, staring anxiously at her. 'You can't open other people's letters.'

'I have a right to open this one,' insisted Anna. 'And you have a right, too, to know what has

37

happened to Mr Springfield. Go and keep watch at the door. As soon as Mr Browser appears, let us know.'

Selwyn obeyed her, partly because he was pleased to be able to move away from the letter and the crime which was about to be committed. Spiky stood at Anna's side, wondering. Girls, he thought, could be much more ruthless than boys, if they'd set their minds on something.

Anna eased the letter from the envelope and opened it out flat. With Spiky peering over her shoulder, she started to read.

'Dear Mr Browser,

You may be wondering why I am writing to you. I know from what Selwyn has often said, that you are a reasonable man and will listen to what other people have to say, even if it is sometimes hard to believe. I can no longer go on fighting alone against something greater than myself. When I go to work tomorrow I shall write a statement informing the authorities of what I know is going on, and I shall send a copy to the police. However, there is a special threat to your school and its children which makes me fear lest damage is done to them before I have been proved right. Sometimes officials can take a long time to act, and there is not all that much time left. Mr Browser, your school lies directly in the path of pollution, and it is the aim of the bearers of pollution to reduce Chivvy Chase School, and then the town, to a place where no one can exist any more. The poison will reach the children by way of the school field, which Selwyn says is already turning brown, by way of the school kitchen, where the food will be affected, and by way of poisoned rain when they are out in the playground. If they succeed in this, then the town of Chivvy Chase will be the next to suffer.

'I have discovered the secret of the polluters, and for this reason I believe my life could be in danger. Mr Browser, the polluters work from Outer Space. They are a race of maggot-like beings who plan to take over the world by spreading their poison over it and so destroying crops and people! These are no monsters with guns – these creatures are much more deadly. What better way of taking over a world than by first making it unfit for its inhabitants? No doubt you have heard about the hole in the sky which scientists have been talking about of late? They believe that the use of poisonous sprays all over the world has weakened the oxygen layer all round the world, and now in one place it is so weak that it amounts to a hole in the sky.

'That's their belief, but, Mr Browser, I have now found out something which I have long suspected – that hole in the sky may have been helped by our own poisons, but it has been mainly caused by poisons coming from the other side of the oxygen layer – from space. The hole has been created by would-be invaders, who wish to conquer our world by first laying it waste and making human life gradually impossible upon it. They have broken through the hole, and are making their first attempts to poison a whole area. They have their agents on Earth, and they visit them at night in transparent floating bubbles which enable them to live in their own atmosphere. I have seen them, Mr Browser, and also seen one of their agents in the woods. They mean to spread their poison in various ways, using rain clouds as a cover for their activities, and even creating clouds themselves when necessary. I am writing about all this to you because I believe they have chosen Chivvy Chase as an area for experiment. From what happens here, they will learn how to proceed against the rest of the world. If you don't believe me, let me tell you what I have seen.

'Why, Mr Browser, has it rained nearly every day for at least the last month at the same time? Why has the climate here become so regular in this respect? Because the polluters send down their cloud capsules, timed to break open at the same time each day and spread their poisonous rain over Chivvy Chase. Has not life become harder in the last month? Aren't all the children more irritable and less cheerful than before? Don't you feel discontented yourself, perhaps even unwell at times? Believe me, Mr Browser, I have seen the cloud capsules dropping gently down in a hollow in the Nature Reserve early in the morning, when the dew is still lying on the dying grass. And yesterday I saw the capsules breaking, and sending up their poisonous fumes to gather in a cloud and move, with or without the wind, over Chivvy Chase School and then on over the town. This happened at twenty-

five past ten, so that at playtime the horrible rain could fall on children and make their symptoms worse.

'Hard to believe, Mr Browser? I fear that people will say that I am mad. But you must believe me, to save all your children! I invite you to come to the Nature Reserve early in the morning, to see for yourself. I believe the Space Maggots must be making use of a disused satellite, which they intend to make their base for sending more and more poison down to Earth. Please, Mr Browser –'

'He's coming!' hissed Selwyn from the door, and Anna stuffed the letter back into the envelope and they all ran for the safety of their seats, Spiky ignoring Michael Fairlie's curious questioning about what he had been doing.

Mr Browser went straight to his table, frowned when he saw the letter lying on it, and put it at once in his pocket. Spiky, Selwyn and Anna, forgetting all else, sat watching him.

'Some of you,' said Mr Browser sternly, 'appear to have forgotten that you should by now have found work to do.'

They took the hint, and opened their books, but this only meant that they were staring blankly at their books instead of at Mr Browser. They were trying to take in all they had read in the letter – and Selwyn was trying to hide his guilt at the opening of it. At the same time Spiky and Anna wondered how they could endure it if Mr Browser tried to keep its contents a secret and never spoke of the cloud capsules to them.

'It's unbelievable!' whispered Spiky to Selwyn, who was sitting behind him.

'But Mr Springfield was a sensible man – and look what's happened to him!' replied Selwyn.

'Was a sensible man? Do you think he's dead?' commented Spiky.

'What's going on?' asked Michael Fairlie, leaning forward in his curiosity.

'Oh, nothing,' answered Spiky, pleased to have the opportunity to tease him.

There the matter might have rested, had not the Headmaster, Mr Sage, come in to speak to Mr Browser.

'What a noisy entrance to school the children made this morning,' he began. 'They seem to be getting worse, in spite of all I've said to them.'

'I did my best,' said Mr Browser, annoyed.

'I know, I know. It's as though they have something in them,' mused Mr Sage – and then Mr Browser took out the letter.

'I was given this first thing this morning by Selwyn Jordan,' he said quietly – so quietly that if Spiky and Selwyn had not been especially concentrating, no one would have heard him. Anna, at the back of the classroom, frantically tried to lip read. 'It's from the Nature Reserve Warden, who disappeared yesterday,' explained Mr Browser.

'Missing, indeed,' said Mr Sage, taking the letter, but determined not to forget why he had come to the classroom.

'It's a strange letter,' added Mr Browser. 'I'll be pleased to hear what you think of it.'

As Mr Sage read the letter his eyebrows rose, and further on he put on an expression which meant that he would have had a low opinion of it if it had been written by a child. At last he came to the end of it.

'This confirms what I've been hearing,' he said. 'I've been told he's gone a bit round the bend about pollution. Has pollution on the brain, I should think.'

'Nevertheless, it's odd that he should have vanished just when he was going to tell the police about it all,' suggested Mr Browser.

'Couldn't face the truth, probably,' declared Mr Sage comfortably. 'Realized no one would believe such nonsense.'

'What do you suggest I do about the letter?' asked Mr Browser, taking it back. Mr Sage smiled, as he sometimes did when children talked nonsense to him.

'If I were you – I'd destroy it,' he said.

'I don't know – it's a kind of cry for help – I think I might go out to the Nature Reserve early tomorrow morning just to make sure the story really is all nonsense,' said Mr Browser thoughtfully. The Headmaster turned away impatiently.

'That's up to you,' he said. 'But don't be late for school – and come and see me at playtime about the general behaviour of the children. I'm holding a short Staff Meeting. You two boys in the front – Selwyn and Simon – get your heads down to some work, will you?'

44

He stalked out of the classroom and shook his head for most of the way along the corridor. Why was Browser sometimes so unrealistic – so out of this world? He would never make a good Headmaster, thought Mr Sage somewhat sadly, and returned to his study to plan what he was going to say to the teachers at playtime.

In the classroom Mr Browser sat at his desk pretending to mark books – but he was making slow progress, as slow as Spiky and Selwyn were with their work. Suddenly Michael Fairlie tapped Selwyn on the shoulder.

'Message from Anna,' he whispered, holding up a piece of paper – but when Selwyn attempted to take it, Michael pulled back his hand and opened it himself. The contents evidently did not excite him much.

'It's only a bet,' he said, and passed the paper over to Selwyn who read: 'Bet you it doesn't rain at playtime – Anna.'

Selwyn passed the note to Spiky, and from then on they were waiting for playtime – and from the way Mr Browser strolled around the classroom and kept on looking out of the windows, it seemed that he was on the lookout too. Work dragged on, and the sky remained clear.

'Quarter of an hour to go,' whispered Selwyn. Spiky made secret signals to Anna, wanting to know how many peppermints she was prepared to lose if it did rain – and still the sky was clear. Five was the most she would go to, and she was beginning to regret them.

The cloud appeared in the sky one minute before the bell for playtime rang, and it looked harmless enough.

'Books closed,' said Mr Browser promptly. He was annoyed to have to spend most of his breaktime in Mr Sage's study. 'Don't hang about anyone. Outside in the sunshine.'

Even as he spoke the sun went behind a cloud. Class 8 hastened into the playground, and at once Spiky and Selwyn were joined by Anna.

'What were Browser and Sage on about?' she asked, and Spiky quickly told her.

'Sage doesn't believe in Mr Springfield's letter,' he said, 'but Browser isn't sure. He said something about going into the Nature Reserve very early tomorrow morning, to see if anything happens.'

'And even if it does, I don't suppose he'll tell us anything about it,' complained Selwyn.

'He won't have to,' burst out Anna.

'Why not?'

'Because if he can go there early, so can we,' she declared. 'Let's go and see for ourselves.'

The boys looked doubtful.

'My mother wouldn't let me out so early,' admitted Selwyn. 'Especially after what's happened.'

'My dad would be suspicious,' added Spiky.

'You do make problems,' said Anna irritably. 'If we all go together, and say that Mr Browser is meeting us there, and that it's a good time to see the wildlife there, they'll grumble, but I bet they let you go.'

Some girls have a nerve, thought Spiky. 'And what happens if Browser sees us?' he asked.

'Then,' said Anna, 'we'll have to confess that we read the letter.'

Spiky looked at her in open admiration. 'I'll come,' he said.

'I will too, if I can,' said Selwyn, 'though my mum won't like me going into the woods again.'

They fell silent as they thought about the hut in the woods once more. Then the first drops of acid rain began to fall, and Mr Browser appeared hastily in the playground, blew his whistle and beckoned them all inside out of the rain.

'Move yourselves!' he said. 'There's no need to get wet.'

'He's awfully excited,' said Anna.

'Five peppermints, please!' demanded Spiky, and grinned all over his face as the raindrops splashed on the playground.

4 Mr Browser's Dawn Patrol

When Mr Browser's alarm clock began buzzing it was still dark. With a great effort of will Mr Browser stumbled out of bed and switched on his bedside lamp. This action completed the waking up process of his wife.

'Surely you don't need to get up yet, George,' she grumbled. 'You won't be able to see anything as early as this.'

'By the time I reach the woods the dawn will be breaking,' answered Mr Browser. 'That's when I'll have most chance of seeing the wildlife unobserved. I shall find out exactly where the creatures live, and when I go there with my class I'll be able to lead the children straight to the animals' lairs.'

'Lairs? Are there wild animals there? Do be careful, George. I think it's ridiculous, the things you do for that school!'

'For the children,' Mr Browser corrected her.

'Same thing,' said his wife. 'I bet you'll never find Mr Sage getting up at five o'clock to go out to the woods.'

'Maybe for a game of golf,' said Mr Browser, but

his wife was in no mood for humour. She snorted and put her head under her duvet.

'I'll make my own breakfast,' said Mr Browser. 'There's no need for you to get up.'

He received no reply to this, and he had to admit to himself as he went to the bathroom that his excuse for visiting the Nature Reserve so early had sounded hard to believe. However, the story achieved for him what he wanted, and after a quick breakfast he drove away in the direction of the woods. He parked his car at a point nearest to the path which led towards the Nature Reserve, and set off on foot towards the gate. The sky was lightening, and the birds were beginning their chorus to greet the dawn.

The Nature Reserve, deep in the woods, was a lonely place where no friendly lights were to be seen, and Mr Browser was grateful for the slow conquest of the darkness by the rising sun. Apart from the singing of the birds, there were secret rustlings and pattering sounds which suggested that he was being watched suspiciously by creatures who didn't expect to see human visitors at that hour.

He was pleased to see that he had found the way to Mr Springfield's hut. It stood there, closed up, like a dead thing in the midst of the life all around it, and Mr Browser shivered as he thought of the man who had so suddenly and mysteriously disappeared from it.

Then he reminded himself that he was here to prove whether the letter he had received had been written by a sane, if desperate man, or by a man

50

driven out of his mind by loneliness. As he stood in front of the hut Mr Browser found it easy to believe that the second possibility was more likely. Yet he must go ahead and prove that it was so, and in order to do so he had to find a hollow somewhere in the woods, and keep on the watch for what the Warden had called 'cloud capsules'.

Mr Browser had not often wandered further into the woods than the bringing of a class to the Warden's hut had required; but once, years back, he had patiently followed a friend who had searched keenly for varieties of plants, and had put Mr Browser to shame by naming about twenty different ones. In the course of that afternoon they had reached a grassy hollow, and now he struck out, as far as he could remember, in that direction.

Squirrels ran across the path in front of him, and birds sprang to one side into the bushes as if he were as dangerous as a passing car. From time to time he had to make decisions as two paths crossed, and still there was no sign of a hollow.

Time was passing, and he began to fear he was lost as he wandered along a number of very similar paths. Now the sun was trying to pierce the darkest parts of the woods with its almost horizontal rays. As he looked upwards something wafted down into the bushes ahead of him – perhaps a feather, thought Mr Browser; it was too early in the year for leaves to be falling from the trees. Further ahead of him similar shapes were descending, gradually drifting from side to side in sloping movements which would bring them gently to the earth. Cloud capsules, thought Mr Browser, and he ran forward, afraid the shapes might disappear before he could reach them.

The path before him opened out into a large, grassy hollow. Yet the hollow was not the green of grass in colour, but a silvery grey, mother-of-pearl shade, formed by thousands of shapes which had come to rest on the grass and were still being joined by a few latecomers – the same kind of shapes which he had seen ahead of him on the path.

Mr Browser moved forward to look more closely at these strange objects, which as he drew near seemed to merge into the ground until he was no longer certain they were there. He bent forward to inspect what now resembled large blobs of dew, when a crashing noise disturbed him. Looking up, he saw the branches of a large bush falling back into place, as if a large animal had just passed between them.

Then, as one of the branches snapped, he glimpsed something green – with straps on it. The 'large animal' was carrying a kind of rucksack on its back! Mr Browser straightened up and charged across the hollow. When he reached the spot where the figure had been, there was no sign of life. In the distance there were sounds as of a man running, but they soon died away, and Mr Browser returned to study the globules which lay on blades of grass and on the ground between them. The blobs looked smaller now, yet more concentrated. Could it be possible that they were disguising themselves as drops of dew?

He was still shaking his head at the strangeness of his idea when he was again disturbed. This time the noise was unmistakable; it was the sound of running feet, coming towards the hollow along the same path he had taken himself. What creatures had he now disturbed?

'Mr Browser!'

'Good morning, Mr Browser!'

'So you did come to see what's happening, Mr Browser!'

The voices were those of Spiky, Selwyn and Anna, and Mr Browser could not have been more taken aback if he had seen a lion, a hippopotamus and a giraffe coming towards him.

'Whatever are you children doing here?' he demanded as they arrived, panting, at his side.

'Same as you are doing, Mr Browser. Looking to see if there are any cloud capsules.'

'Cloud capsules? How do you know about them?' asked Mr Browser, staring hard at Spiky. Anna spoke up.

'It's really my fault, Mr Browser. I read the letter from Mr Springfield which was on your desk – and we want to know what happened to him and what's going on.'

Mr Browser looked at them hard and long.

'Yes, I suppose you have a kind of right to be curious,' he admitted – and all three relaxed at once. 'But how did you persuade your parents to allow you out so early? I hope you haven't come out at this hour without telling them.'

'Oh no, Mr Browser,' said Anna sweetly. 'We told them that you were taking a few of us to look at the Nature Reserve early in the morning, because it's the best time to be in the woods!'

'Oh, did you?' said Mr Browser, wondering how much more trouble his dawn patrol might cause him.

'Have you seen anything, Mr Browser?' asked Selwyn. 'Any capsules falling from the sky, I mean?'

'Well, I –' Mr Browser hesitated and looked down to the ground.

'The ground's covered with capsules,' said Spiky, following Mr Browser's gaze.

'That's morning dew, isn't it?' put in Anna.

'Too big,' declared Selwyn, 'and too silvery looking.'

'You saw them fall, Mr Browser?' asked Spiky accusingly.

'Well – er – yes, some of them,' admitted Mr Browser, annoyed to be questioned by children as a teacher questions children. Yet he was inclined to think that they deserved to know the truth. 'They were still falling when I arrived, and looked much bigger.'

'There you are, Spiky, I knew we'd miss something because you couldn't get up out of bed quickly enough,' said Anna.

'Did you see anyone else here?' asked Selwyn.

'I glimpsed somebody rushing into the woods,' said Mr Browser. 'That is, all I saw was the rucksack on his back.'

'That's the same man as we saw,' declared Anna. 'He ran off between the trees. He was like a tramp, with a rucksack on his back.'

Mr Browser looked questioningly at her, and she answered his question before he could speak.

'Oh no, it wasn't Mr Springfield,' she said. 'It was a short man with a beard and hairs all over his face.'

'Maybe he knows something about what's going on,' said Selwyn. 'There's something odd about these little round objects – they remind me of the bits of mercury I saw when Spiky broke the thermometer at school.'

'Mercury!' said Mr Browser, looking closely at some of the globules. 'Mercury can play a part in poisoning the land – and people. That and too many nitrates – I wonder, I wonder!'

'What do you wonder, Mr Browser?' asked Anna.

Mr Browser looked up, as if for a few moments he had forgotten all about the presence of the children.

'I was wondering if what Mr Springfield wrote in his letter could be true,' he said, 'but it sounds so unlikely. I wish I'd been able to speak to the man who ran away –'

'I'll try and find out where he is,' said Spiky. 'Maybe if I catch up with him he'll be able to tell us something.'

Spiky, always ready for action, suddenly shot off along the path by which they had come.

'I'll go too,' Anna called after him, but Mr Browser grabbed her by the arm. 'Come back, Simon!' he

56

shouted. 'I don't want you all running off into the woods,' he told Anna. 'I'm sure that tramp will have disappeared by now, and Simon will be back in a few moments.'

Spiky had either not heard his call or had preferred to ignore it, and had disappeared round a bend in the path.

'You'd do better to help me collect a few of these objects,' went on Mr Browser. 'Find me a few of the biggest – I want to take them away and try and find out what they're made of. Have either of you something I can carry them in?'

Selwyn produced a bag with a few sweets in it.

'Have one each,' he said, 'and then we can use the empty bag.'

Anna bent over the ground, choosing the largest of the round objects she could find. With one finger she tried to roll it into the palm of her other hand.

'Ow!' she cried, dropping it as if it were a burning match. 'That stings!'

She held out her hand and showed Mr Browser a small red patch where the globule had rested.

'Acid,' said Mr Browser. 'Acid as well! These things have most of the ingredients required for pollution! I shall have to ask my friend Mr Benchley at the Comprehensive School to analyse them. Take great care, both of you, that you don't touch any of them with your bare hands. Find me a big leaf, or a stick, Selwyn, so that I can put them in the bag without touching them.'

It was Anna who found a large laurel leaf which Mr Browser used to persuade some of the globules into the paper bag.

'That's enough,' he decided after a while. 'We'd better start back now. There's time for you both to go home first if you want to.'

'No, thank you,' said Anna. 'I told my parents I'd be going straight to school with you, Mr Browser.'

'So did I,' said Selwyn.

'We'll do that then,' agreed Mr Browser. 'I'll take

you back to the school playground, and then I'll nip across to the Comprehensive School and find Mr Benchley. He's usually there early. But first of all we'd better collect Simon. He can't have found the tramp, or he'd be back by now.'

'If we walk along the path, we'll probably meet him coming back,' said Anna.

'We'll start off and go a little way, but we'd better not move too far from here, just in case he comes back another way,' said Mr Browser, and as he moved off he cupped his hands to the sides of his mouth and shouted.

'Simon! Hurry up, we're going!' And Anna pierced the silence of the woods with the cry: 'Spiky! Spike – eeeeey, where are you?'

So Mr Browser decided that Spiky would probably answer most easily to his nickname, and he, too, yelled out, 'Spike – eeeeey!'

There was still no answer, and there was silence in the woods as the birds listened to these unusual cries.

5 Secret Agent of the Space Maggots

When Spiky Jackson ran off in search of the tramp, he had little hope of finding him. Spiky's restless nature was not made for patient study, and the careful methods of detection of a Sherlock Holmes were not for him. So when Mr Browser began to fuss over the little silvery globules on the grass, and it became clear that nothing dramatic was about to happen, he seized on the chance to run through the woods in the slight hope of finding adventure.

After five minutes he reached the place where the tramp had disappeared into the trees. He swerved off the path and headed in the direction he believed the man had taken. At first he charged through the undergrowth like a hunted animal, but after tripping a couple of times and suffering from the attentions of a stinging nettle, he slowed down gradually and came to a halt. He was swiftly losing enthusiasm for the chase – probably, he thought, the tramp has gone off to the town in order to beg or buy something for his breakfast.

Something made a rustling sound in the woods near him, and made him wish he had someone with him.

The noise could surely not have been made by a wild animal – there were no dangerous wild animals in the woods, he tried to convince himself. Foxes, perhaps, but a fox would be unlikely to attack a human being – or would it?

Surprised by his own nervousness, he turned back towards the path.

'Stay there!' called out a gruff voice, and a large hand seized him tightly by the arm.

'Let me go!' cried Spiky, swinging round to see the hairy face and glittering eyes of the same tramp for whom he had been searching.

'Keep quiet!' the tramp warned him, tweaking his arm viciously. 'Or I'll keep you quiet! Come with me, and don't try to run away, or it'll be the worse for you!'

Spiky could only obey him, for that grip was like iron, and the tramp's eyes shone with a kind of desperation that was frightening to behold.

'Where are you taking me?' Spiky dared to ask.

'Only to a quiet place where we won't be disturbed,' said the tramp, 'and where you can tell me what you and your friends are doing in the woods at this time!'

He pushed Spiky between a bush and a tree, and Spiky found himself in a shady hide-away, in which there were tins of food, a groundsheet – and the rucksack which Mr Browser had mentioned.

'Sit down!' ordered the tramp, and flung him to the ground. As Spiky pulled himself into a sitting position, the tramp stood over him in a threatening manner, and Spiky had the chance to look more closely at him. He was not as old a man as Spiky had at first thought. With a shave, a wash and some combing of his straggly hair, he could look as young as Spiky's father, or even younger. His skin, beneath the hair and the dirt, was pale, and his expression, now that he had calmed down a little, seemed more one ruled by fear than anger. Not that this comforted Spiky much, because he knew he was in the hands of an excitable and perhaps desperate person, who might become violent if angered.

'Now – what are you doing, hanging about in the woods so early? Are you with that man I saw in the hollow just now? The truth, mind, or it'll be the worse for you!'

'Yes, we are with him,' said Spiky. 'He's our teacher, and we've come to look at the woods in the early morning.'

'No!' said the tramp in a low voice. 'That's not the truth. Nobody would bring children here at this hour to study plants. Besides, I saw him looking at –'

'At what?' asked Spiky, something of his usual spirit returning.

'Never you mind!' the tramp replied threateningly. 'I know that man is up to something, and until you tell me the truth, you can be sure I shan't be letting you go. It doesn't matter to me, you know, whether you ever leave this wood!'

The threat was clear, and Spiky decided it was time to tell at least some of the truth.

'We are here,' he said, 'because we know about the disappearance of Mr Springfield, the Warden, and we want to find out more about it.'

The tramp looked troubled.

'How much do you know?' he asked, and turned for a moment to look behind him.

'Mr Springfield wrote a letter to our teacher and told him the woods were being used in order to poison the town – and firstly our school and grounds, as a sort of experiment to see whether the human race could be wiped out. I don't understand it at all, but Mr Springfield told Mr Browser to come to the hollow and see for himself.'

'So the secret is out!' muttered the tramp, looking paler than before. 'Has your Mr Browser told anyone else about the letter?'

'I don't think so,' said Spiky. 'But if he finds something suspicious, he'll have to tell the police, I suppose. There isn't anything to discover, though, is there?'

'Boy,' said the tramp, 'you have chanced upon happenings which have ruined my life. I wasn't always like this, you know. Once I was a respectable man, but then I fell into bad ways, and then – they seized upon me and made me their slave.'

'They? Who?' asked Spiky, forgetting his own fear enough to have some pity for the tramp.

'Creatures that are trying to endanger the world. Pollutants, they call themselves, but I call them Space Maggots. I've seen them – they look like huge maggots, or sea horses, but it's not easy to describe them in detail, because when I saw them each one was floating in a transparent ball, to protect them against the germs and viruses they might meet with on Earth.'

'How could such creatures conquer the Earth?' asked Spiky.

'More easily than you might think, boy. The trouble is, you're used to thinking about monsters and huge space craft sending out lethal rays to destroy us – all very fine for stories, but these creatures are much more deadly. They plan to kill off all life on Earth by slowly poisoning it – by sending clouds to pollute the air and rain to pollute the water. Then, when no one is left alive, they'll come down and take charge of everything with no trouble at all. Those little silver balls your teacher was looking at are part of their experiment. They have been sending a cloud of poisonous rain over your school and the town at a certain time each day, and with the help of their agents they will find out how long it is going to take to bring the world as we know it to a halt. Already the grass on your school field is dying, and the children and teachers are growing restless and irritated. The same thing is beginning to happen in the town, too.'

'If they have agents, who are they?' asked Spiky. 'They should tell the rest of us what is going on, so that we can stop it.'

'Not so easy,' said the tramp, smiling. 'I know, because I am one of their agents. Besides sending down the poisonous capsules, they are sending me a wonderful drug without which I can no longer live. They have me in their power, boy, and many people like me, and there's little I can do about it. If I were to fail to help them, I'd be finished. Just like the Warden of the Nature Reserve.'

'Finished? What do you mean?' demanded Spiky, and the tramp shrugged his shoulders.

'It would only need one or two of those capsules to finish me off,' he said.

'But what about the Warden?' asked Spiky. 'What's happened to him?'

Again the tramp looked uneasily over his shoulder.

'Come with me,' he said after some hesitation, and turning again, pushed his way through several thick bushes, holding the branches back so that Spiky could follow him. 'There he is,' he said. Spiky bent forward, and saw the body of the Warden lying on a carpet of leaves and ferns, bound up with ropes.

'Is he dead?' he asked.

'No, unconscious.'

As if to prove this true, the Warden moved his head and gave a muffled groan.

'Why have you done this?' demanded Spiky. 'You can't keep him tied up like that for long –'

'I am waiting for further orders,' said the tramp. 'They made me do it. Only when he becomes their slave will they set him free.'

Spiky turned away and the tramp grabbed his arm.

'Oh no, you don't run away,' he said. 'I shall now

have to find out what my masters would like me to do with you.'

He pushed Spiky back to the open space where his rucksack lay, and thrust him to the ground. Then he opened the rucksack and took out a metal object, which Spiky thought might be a kind of lamp or a camera.

'What's that for?' he asked anxiously.

'It's part of the kit which these creatures give to their agents. It sends out rays which enable them to focus their capsules on the point at which they are to land. And when it's time for them to form into a cloud, the rays can be used to help activate them if the sun's not strong enough.'

Spiky made a move to inspect the lamp-shaped object, but the tramp roughly thrust him back.

'Oh no you don't!' he said. 'I shall need that to warn them that their plans have partly been made known.'

'When will you do that?'

'When I help set the cloud in motion. Their satellite will be orbiting just above us at that time, and I'll be able to contact them easily.'

'How?' asked Spiky, whose questions were partly put out of curiosity and partly because he hoped they would at least delay the tramp from sudden violence.

'Have you heard of the heliograph?' asked the tramp.

'It means sending signals by lamp, doesn't it?'

'That's right. Well, this isn't exactly heliographing, but it's something similar.'

'Thank you for telling me,' said Spiky, pleased to find the tramp appeared to have calmed down. 'May I go now? I don't want to be late for school.'

The tramp laughed, and his thin lips turned the laugh into such a sneer that Spiky shivered again.

'I should let you go, should I? And straight away you'd be telling people where the Warden is, for a start. No, you have to come with me, and I shall tell my masters about you, and we'll see what they decide is to be done with you.'

'But you're holding me here against my will! You could be put in prison for that. It's kidnapping!'

Again the tramp laughed.

'I'm afraid it's a question of you or me,' he said. 'You don't yet understand the power of these creatures. If I let you go, and they discover that you know too much, my life wouldn't be worth much.'

'I don't believe in these Space Maggots of yours – they're just inside your head,' said Spiky desperately.

'Inside and outside,' observed the tramp. 'You will believe in them before long. Come to think of it, you look a promising sort of lad to be the first boy agent for them, devoting the rest of your life to spreading untidiness and dirt, helping to pollute the water and kill the grass and –'

'Spiky! Spike – eeeey!' A high-pitched voice, which Spiky at once recognized as Anna's, penetrated the woods and silenced the tramp.

Spiky sat up straight, and the tramp instantly sprang at him and pressed his hand over his mouth.

'Not a word!' he whispered. 'Not a sound, or your time is up!'

'Hurry up, Spiky, we're going!' came Anna's voice again, followed by Selwyn's fainter tones.

'Spiky – where are you?'

Mr Browser joined in the cries, and it was clear that they were walking up and down the path and calling out from different positions in the hope of gaining an answer. Spiky's mouth was hurting under the constant pressure of the tramp's hand. For a while the voices became louder – Anna and Selwyn were perhaps pointing out where they had seen the tramp leave the path, thought Spiky. His hopes rose a little, but then the voices faded away. The tramp waited for a long while – perhaps as long as five minutes, though it seemed much longer to Spiky, before he at last took his hand from the boy's mouth.

'They've gone,' he said, and looked at his watch. 'It's nearly eight o'clock, so we have two and a quarter hours almost before the capsules are supposed to be set free. We'll go nearer to the hollow, so that we can watch in case anybody else comes along.'

'What about the Warden?' asked Spiky.

'We'll find out about him,' replied the tramp. He picked up the rucksack and put it on his back, grabbed Spiky's arm and urged him out of the hideout. Then they began a long trek through the woods, never on a path, in places where Spiky had never been before. Half an hour went by before they came in sight of the hollow, and then Spiky realized that he was viewing it from the opposite side of the woods. They had reached it by a roundabout way which had offered the tramp the most safety from possible detection.

'Now,' he said, 'we shall wait until I can communicate with my masters, and they will tell me what is to be done with you and the Warden.'

'You can't do anything to me!' said Spiky desperately. 'People will come to find me – Mr Browser will tell the police, and you'll be arrested.'

'That's all of no importance,' said the tramp,

shaking his head. 'Soon all of us will be in the power of these creatures, so what happens to me and you and the Warden matters very little.'

'Then why don't you let me go?'

'Because while they still need me I'm safe,' said the tramp. 'It may not be for much longer, but I may as well make the most of it. Maybe they'll even preserve me because I've helped them.'

'You're mad!' said Spiky, and put his head in his hands as he sat with his back to an oak tree. 'I think you're making all this up, just to frighten me. If you're so sure of what's happening, you ought to be ashamed of yourself. You ought to be trying to save Chivvy Chase School and the people of the town, not helping alien creatures to destroy everything!'

For a moment the tramp seemed disturbed, but he quickly turned away from Spiky and began to pull the strange machine out of the rucksack.

'I need the drugs they send me,' he muttered. 'I'm going to try and contact them now. I don't like hanging about here with you, in case they send out a search party for you.'

'Which they will,' said Spiky with pretended confidence. Even if they do, he thought, they'll be unlikely to find me here.

The tramp now had the lamp-like object on the ground and was setting it on a low tripod which formed a circle into which the 'lamp' fitted comfortably, pointing upwards. Spiky leaned across to inspect it more closely. Instead of a lens, scores of tiny strips criss-crossed over the face of it, and down the side were several switches. The material was light, for the tramp picked it up easily in one hand, and grabbed Spiky with the other.

'Come into the hollow with me. I'm going to start signalling. Maybe the satellite is close enough over-head to be able to receive my signals.'

They didn't go to the centre of the hollow, for the tramp was very nervous about being seen. He soon set the tripod on the ground and swivelled the 'lamp' around until he had it pointing to his satisfaction. Then he began pressing one of the switches, which moved backwards and forwards according to the amount of pressure he put on it.

From the side Spiky could see that the 'lamp' was glowing in various shades of red. After a while the tramp switched it off, and the glow died away.

'Were you signalling?' asked Spiky, and the tramp nodded. After a while he pressed the switch again, and went through the same procedure. This time, after he had switched off and the red glow had died away again, suddenly the glow was there of its own accord, and the tramp watched the thin strips as they changed colour, ending in a bright red which looked capable of burning the strips away. The tramp stared at the tripod as if hypnotized.

'What did that mean?' asked Spiky, seeing that for the first time the tramp looked scared.

'I don't understand it at all,' he mumbled, 'but one

71

thing is clear – they are coming to investigate for themselves, and they want the capsules to remain unbroken until they can organize the sending of the cloud themselves. I think I can guess what that might mean.'

Now the tramp was beginning to shiver, with the shivering of a man about to suffer an attack of malaria or some other terrible fever.

'So what will happen?' asked Spiky.

'It means that they will strengthen the poisonous effect of the capsules, so that all those who know anything about their secrets will certainly be killed. Probably they'll send down more capsules, much stronger than those already lying here.'

'But that could mean that all of us might die,' said Spiky.

'All who come in contact with the poisonous cloud which will seek them out wherever they are!'

'You can't let that happen!' cried Spiky.

'I can't stop it,' replied the tramp with a wry smile. 'You still don't understand, son, we're all powerless against these Space Maggots.'

'Then why don't we run, and try to save ourselves?'

'No good,' said the tramp. 'Besides, they may just decide not to kill me – they may take me away somewhere else to start my work as an agent afresh. Yes, they might preserve the people who are useful to them.'

'What about me? Let me go!' Spiky stood up, but the tramp was too quick for him.

'You are one of those who know too much. If I let you go, I shall certainly suffer for it myself.'

Spiky sat down again in order to free himself from the tramp's painful grip. Still he tried to cling to the hope that the tramp was a madman – though there was little real comfort in that for him. The tramp withdrew the tripod from the edge of the hollow, and forced Spiky back into the shelter of the trees. There Spiky made one last appeal for his freedom.

'If we're all going to die anyway, what's the difference if you hold me here or not?'

The tramp appeared to be thinking about this, but Spiky quickly saw from the hardening expression on his face that the attempt had failed.

'You are my hostage –' he began, but stopped when he realized that Spiky was no longer looking at him, but beyond him to the hollow.

'Look what's floating down!' said Spiky. 'More capsules!'

The tramp turned to look.

'Yes, and bigger ones,' he said. 'The attack is beginning!'

The capsules, again a silvery grey colour, but this time larger than greatcoat buttons, were making their swaying descent to earth. There were so many of them that Spiky had to look away, or he would have become dizzy watching them. The first of them had reached the ground when he looked up again, to see the tramp staring as if hypnotized into the sky. Spiky followed his gaze, and saw what it was that had so overcome the tramp.

Above the cloud capsules, a giant capsule was floating, a transparent bubble that appeared and disappeared in the changing light. In the bubble from time to time a shape appeared – a shape like a huge, watery maggot. Though as horrified by it as Spiky was, the tramp seemed in a strange way to be drawn towards it and began to move out from the cover of the trees.

'What do you want of me?' Spiky heard the tramp mumbling.

The bubble came down to the height of the tallest trees – and then the instinct for survival broke into Spiky's trance-like state, and he turned and ran. He expected the tramp to come after him, but nothing happened. He crashed on between the trees, heedless of where he was going, only wishing to remove himself from that horrible shape in the bubble. In his panic he returned once to the edge of the hollow, and saw the bubble standing in the middle of it and the tramp passing the signalling equipment into it.

Now Spiky had a better idea of his bearings, and skirting the edge of the hollow, he reached the path which led out of the woods. He ran without stopping, praying that the stitch in his side from which he so often suffered would be spared him in this emergency. But no – the pain in his side increased, and his lungs seemed to be bursting, so that he had to come to a dead stop. Fearfully, as he gasped for breath and doubled up to rid himself of the pain, he looked back, dreading lest the tramp or even the horrible creature in the bubble might be following him.

The path was empty, and when he looked forward he could see the gate which led out of the Nature Reserve ahead of him. For his own sake and for that of Chivvy Chase School he took a deep breath, stood up straight and began to run again.

And there in front of him, as if he had dropped from the sky, stood the tramp. Exhausted, Spiky stood still in dismay.

'Foolish boy,' said the tramp. 'You're coming back with me. We can't have you warning everybody about what's going to happen!'

Meekly Spiky allowed himself to be pulled and pushed all the way back to the hollow – and overhead, above the trees, a large bubble wavered along with them.

6 The Poison Capsules

For some time Mr Browser, Anna and Selwyn walked up and down the woodland path calling out to Spiky, but when there was no response at all Mr Browser became worried about the strange capsules in his pocket, lest they should disappear.

'It looks as though he's gone back to school,' he said. 'I think we'd better follow him, so that I can contact Mr Benchley and have these capsules examined. Simon is a real nuisance, running off on his own like that. I must say it's typical of him, though.'

'I think it's odd,' said Anna. 'Stupid of him to come all the way out here and then suddenly run away. Spike – eeeeey!' she called once again just for luck but there was no answer, and she tagged on behind the others as they walked back to the gate of the Nature Reserve, through the woods and out to the road which led to Chivvy Chase School.

'Eight o'clock,' said Mr Browser. 'It's a bit early for Mr Benchley to be there, so we'll go back to school first and see if Spiky's there.'

'What if he isn't?' asked Anna.

'Then probably he will have gone home first for a bite of breakfast,' replied Mr Browser.

The school playground was deserted, but the main door was open, and the faint squeak of mops being pushed over the floors of the classrooms could be heard. Mr Watchett, the caretaker, who enjoyed being in charge of the school at such times, came quickly out of a classroom to see who had invaded the school so early.

'Why, Mr Browser,' he said. 'You're very early. You don't want these children inside the building yet, do you?'

Quite clearly Mr Watchett didn't want them inside, and Mr Browser was not one to offend him unnecessarily.

'We were looking for a boy,' he said. 'Spiky – er, Simon Jackson. You haven't seen him, I suppose?'

'I'd know that one if I saw him,' declared Mr Watchett, still looking sternly at Anna and Selwyn. 'He's not in the school, Mr Browser.'

'Thank you. You two had better wait in the playground, and if you see Simon, please come and let me know.'

Selwyn and Anna reluctantly went outside, Mr Watchett returned to his mop and bucket, and Mr Browser went to the Staffroom to read the letter from Mr Springfield once more, and to take a quick look at the capsules in the paper bag. They were still there, quite unchanged, showing that they couldn't be dew-drops, which would by now have soaked into the paper. Mr Browser left the Staffroom and climbed the stairs to the upper floor of the school, where he stood at a window which overlooked the drive-in to the Comprehensive School. He stayed there for ten minutes before he saw what he had been waiting for – Mr Benchley's red car turned into the drive. Mr Browser hurried downstairs and out of the front door.

Selwyn and Anna were hanging about there.

'Spiky hasn't come yet!' called out Anna. Mr Browser made no reply, but her words made him move faster down the path and across the road to the Comprehensive School. Suppose something had happened to the boy, and he hadn't left the woods after all?

He found Mr Benchley in his laboratory, setting out some equipment ready for an experiment.

'Morning, Stan,' said Mr Browser, and took the paper bag from his pocket.

'Morning, George. Fancy seeing you here. Have you come to offer me a sweet?'

'No, no!' replied Mr Browser, not in the mood for jokes. 'I've brought some curious objects across because I'd like you to tell me what they're made of, if you can.'

Mr Benchley looked in the bag and sniffed. He was a frequent sniffer, probably because of all the fumes he'd lived with in the lab. over the years.

'Tip 'em out here,' he said, producing a little metal saucer, and Mr Browser obeyed. 'I haven't much time to spare,' went on Mr Benchley. 'I've quite a complicated experiment to prepare for the Sixth Form.'

'I'd be grateful for any information,' said Mr Browser humbly.

After a few moments the chemistry master appeared to have forgotten all about his own important experiment. He was fascinated, he was puzzled, he was worried by the little objects on which he was carrying out various tests. He put one of them in a test tube and added several different solutions to it. Another one he put in a crucible and heated it up. Litmus paper was used, and after all his efforts he looked most seriously at Mr Browser.

'Don't tell me one of your children brought them to school, George!' he said sternly.

'No,' replied Mr Browser. 'There are thousands of these in the Nature Reserve – I've just been there with three of my children. What do you make of them?'

'They could be highly dangerous,' declared the chemistry master. 'If it's true that there are thousands of them, you must ring the police. If you don't do it, I will. These things contain a curious mixture of mercury and acids – and one or two ingredients I can't identify. Poisonous, they are. Highly poisonous, I'd say. I think a specialist should have a look at them as soon as possible. What are you going to do?'

'I'll ring the police,' said Mr Browser, looking pale. 'One of my pupils may still be in the woods, and I know where the rest of these objects are – so I think it's my responsibility.'

'Good,' said Mr Benchley, relief showing on his face. 'Tell them what I've said – and don't let anybody swallow that stuff. I should think a few of them would be enough to kill somebody.'

'I wonder,' said Mr Browser, thinking of Mr Springfield. 'Thanks, Stan. I'll let you know what happens.'

He hurried back to Chivvy Chase School, and this time he attracted the attention of Anna and Selwyn, who were in the playground with other children.

'Has Simon turned up yet?' he asked.

'Not yet, Mr Browser. Shall I send him in when he comes?' asked Anna.

'Yes, do,' replied Mr Browser, but a sinking feeling inside him reflected the fact that he would now be rather surprised if Spiky did appear. He rushed to the phone in the office and dialled the police. Mr Sage came in while he was telephoning.

'Ringing the police?' said Mr Sage. 'What's all this about?'

Mr Browser explained and Mr Sage sank into a chair.

'Oh no! Not more trouble!' he complained with a groan. 'What with the swimming pool leaking, and Miss Copewell being unwell –'

'All that,' declared Mr Browser, 'could be as nothing compared to this!'

Mr Sage was so surprised by the determination with which Mr Browser said this that he went straight to his room and closed the door. He sat at his desk for some time thinking about the capsules which Mr

Browser had been talking about on the phone, and he recalled that Mr Browser was quite right in saying that the school field was turning a mysterious brown and that playtime had been cancelled on many occasions lately because of rain. Probably just chance behaviour, he thought, but then he remembered too, that he had taken part in a silly argument that morning with his wife, simply because his boiled egg was too lightly done. Everybody was becoming more and more irritable, Mr Browser had said, and judging by his own behaviour and that of the children, Mr Sage couldn't simply declare that this was nonsense and dismiss it from his mind.

Suppose Browser was right and, a cloud far more poisonous could be on its way that morning? Should he send the children home already? No, they had been sent home too often for other reasons lately – and their parents would be out and the children might wander about in the streets and be worse off than if they were confined in school. And what of that annoying boy Simon Jackson, who might still be wandering about in the woods, directly in the path of the oncoming cloud? Mr Sage shrugged his shoulders. He could only hope that the police arrived soon, or that Simon himself arrived, or that somehow the threat of the poisonous cloud were to be proved false. Meanwhile, he decided, his first duty was to the children at school, and he set off to find the caretaker, Mr Watchett, and tell him that as soon as it appeared likely to rain he was to shut and lock all the doors and windows in the corridors.

Later, the teachers must be told to keep all their classroom windows closed.

He was trying to explain what he wanted to the puzzled Mr Watchett when a child came running to find him and tell him that the police had arrived and would like to speak to him. He hurried back to his room, and found Mr Browser and four men in plain clothes waiting for him. One of the detectives was known to him, and he spoke first.

'Good morning, Mr Sage. We've come to talk to Mr Browser, and he suggested that you would like to know what is going on. Indeed, it could be a most important matter for Chivvy Chase School.'

'So I gather, gentlemen,' replied Mr Sage. 'Please do come in.'

When, with some difficulty, Mr Sage had settled them all in his study, the detective introduced his companions.

'These gentlemen,' he said, indicating two of them, 'are members of Special Branch from London. The news of what's happening in Chivvy Chase is causing some alarm there.'

'Have you any news of Mr Springfield?' asked the Headmaster, as though that must be the most likely reason for their presence.

'We can find no clues, beyond the fact that there was a struggle. His disappearance is just one disturbing aspect of the affair.'

'Who could have attacked him?' asked Mr Sage.

'We don't know,' answered the detective, 'but the

phone call from Mr Browser indicated that the re-
sponsible person may still be in the area. Without any
more delay, I think we had better listen most carefully
to what Mr Browser has to say.'

So Mr Browser spoke, and produced his remaining
capsules, which one of the men from London eagerly
but cautiously took, putting them into a small bottle.
When the whole tale was finished, everyone looked
extremely grave, so that Mr Sage became more and
more uneasy.

'If the poison cloud is sent over at the same time as

usual,' said the detective, 'we have an hour or two in which to try and save the boy Jackson and find out what the tramp is up to. Mr Sage, we leave the care of the children to you – see that no one at all is exposed to the poisonous rain if it comes. We will send two police cars to the area of the Nature Reserve as soon as possible, in the hope of preventing the worst. Mr Browser and the two children should come with us, to help us find the danger area as quickly as possible and to aid our attempt to discover the missing boy. We shall, of course, do all we can to prevent them from exposing themselves to any danger. Meanwhile we'll have these capsules analysed, and a report will at once be sent to London. I must tell you, Mr Sage, that this business could be far more serious than you think. It's not just a matter of the attack on one man, but of a planned attack on Chivvy Chase School and then the town itself. This may well be the beginning of an invasion of earth by aliens aiming to render it helpless by polluting it. We don't want to panic the general population, but we may have to send cars around warning people of a poisonous leak from an unknown factory. Please don't tell anyone else of what you know. London will have to decide what our policy will be – and no doubt checks will be made on all satellites circling the earth, to see if any one of them has changed its orbit. Now we must waste no more time. Mr Browser, please collect those two children at once. I shall phone for reinforcements immediately, if I may use your phone, Mr Sage.'

'Of course, of course,' said Mr Sage, who had managed to turn paler than he usually was. 'Why did this have to happen here!' he complained, looking as though he would have liked to blame Mr Browser for it all. 'On a day when my secretary, Miss Copewell, is away ill, too! Well, I suppose I'd better go and ring the bell.'

Nobody was listening to him. Mr Bowser was making for the playground to find Anna and Selwyn, and the officials made for their cars while the detective phoned his headquarters.

'Mr Browser! Mr Browser!' cried Anna when she saw him in the playground. 'Spiky isn't back yet. What do you think has happened to him?'

Mr Browser groaned, for he dreaded to think what might have become of Spiky.

'Fetch Selwyn at once,' he told her. 'We have to show the police where Spiky was when we last saw him.'

Anna darted off in zigzags between the playing children, and as he waited Mr Browser looked up into the sunny sky. There was hardly a cloud to be seen, and those that were there looked harmless and white, and floated like bubbles wafted from a sorcerer's pipe. The sound of a siren from an approaching police car stopped his sky-gazing, and when the car turned in at the gates of Chivvy Chase School it brought him face to face once more with the dangers ahead, and he waved urgently as Anna and Selwyn threaded their way between the children towards him.

7   Battle of the Bubbles

Mr Browser, Anna and Selwyn were hustled into the newly arrived police car, in which none other than the Chief of Police for the whole county was sitting. The men from the Home Office sped off in the direction of London, and two police cars raced off in the opposite direction, with sirens wailing and the children of Chivvy Chase School pressing their noses against the railings and cheering.

That was their last moment of fresh air for that morning, for Mr Sage appeared in the playground himself, blew his whistle and had them all in school before the last stroke of nine had been struck by the church clock. As soon as they were inside, Mr Watchett made a tour of the building, closing all the doors. The puzzled teachers had to make sure that all the windows were firmly shut, and Chivvy Chase School was like a fortress.

The police cars forced their way along the woodland path which led to the Nature Reserve, and, when the gate was opened, drove as far as the Warden's hut.

'We'd better walk from here,' said Mr Browser.

'The boy might be wandering about on any of these paths. It's just possible that he's lost himself.'

But the Chief of Police, now that he was in the wood, seemed not to be so concerned about Spiky.

'Show us at once where you found the capsules,' he demanded. 'Once we have located them – if they're still there – we can look for the boy afterwards.'

Mr Browser looked upset, but there was no arguing with the Chief of Police, who walked so fast that Anna and Selwyn had to trot in order to keep pace with him and tell him which way to turn.

'This is where we saw the the tramp,' said Anna. 'He ran off that way, between the trees.'

'Did he?' said the Chief of Police, as much as to say he had much more important affairs on his mind than the wanderings of a tramp. So Anna and Selwyn kept quiet, and allowed Mr Browser to direct the policemen on the last part of the journey to the hollow. They were not far from it when Selwyn, who had by chance looked upwards through a space between the trees, suddenly stopped.

'Something's following us!' he said, and his voice was earnest enough for everyone to stop and look at him.

'I see nothing,' said the detective, and the Chief of Police looked sharply at Selwyn.

'Who is following us?' he demanded.

'Not who,' said Selwyn. 'What. It was a kind of bubble, with something white in it, and it was floating over the trees above our heads. I saw it for a moment in the gap.'

The Chief of Police had no time for bubbles floating over his head.

'That's the second time you children have tried to delay me,' he said. 'We must push on and find these capsules, if they really do exist.'

'We're not far off,' said Mr Browser. 'I suggest we move as quietly as we can, in case anybody else is in the hollow.'

'Who else could be?' asked one of the policemen, and Anna bit the end of her tongue in stopping herself from suggesting it might be possible for the tramp or Spiky to have gone there.

'There's the hollow!' said Mr Browser. 'And Spiky and the tramp are there!'

'Told you so!' whispered Anna, and then re-membered she hadn't spoken her thoughts.

'Quiet!' demanded the Chief of Police. 'All of you keep out of sight, behind trees, and my men spread out on either side so that should we want to capture this man we can approach him from several directions. Mr Browser, is that the man you saw?'

'That's his rucksack on the ground,' replied Mr Browser. 'Look at that strange camera-like contrap-tion he has in one hand. And in the other he's holding Simon Jackson by the collar!'

'That's him!' said Anna. 'Isn't it, Selwyn? And there's someone else there lying on the ground! Why, I think it's a man, tied up –'

'That's Mr Springfield!' whispered Selwyn. 'He looks very still – I hope he's all right!'

'You'd be still, if you were tied up like that,' declared Anna.

'Quiet, you children,' ordered the Chief of Police. 'Do you think that's the Warden, Mr Browser?'

'Yes,' said Mr Browser. 'He has the same colour hair. And if Selwyn recognizes him, then I'm sure.'

'Are you sure, boy?' asked the Chief of Police.

'Certain,' answered Selwyn.

'This is a curious affair,' said one of the detectives. 'Why should a tramp like that tie up the Warden and drag him to the middle of the hollow, and kidnap the boy as well?'

'Because –' began Anna, but Selwyn interrupted her.

'Look up in the sky,' he whispered. 'That's why the tramp has come here. I can see several of those bubble things.'

The Chief of Police frowned at him, but then he followed with his eyes the direction in which Selwyn was pointing, and to his surprise he saw two of the bubble things hovering overhead, and had to hold on to the trunk of a tree to try and recover from the shock. Inside the bubbles were strange white shapes, a cross between sea horses, knights on a chess board and maggots.

'It's true!' muttered the Chief of Police.

'It's an invasion!' whispered Selwyn.

'They're coming for Spiky and the Warden!' said Anna, turning pale.

The Chief of Police stood up straight and remembered that he was the Chief of Police.

'Quiet! Nobody is to move, or their attention may be attracted,' he ordered. 'P.C. Nixon, you're armed and the fate of all of us may depend on you. Be ready to shoot down those bubbles if they try to land. Be ready to take the children and run, Mr Browser.'

Spiky must have seen the bubbles too, for he tried suddenly to wrench himself away from the tramp.

'Stay where you are!' the tramp threatened him in a loud, frightened voice. 'I'm going to send signals out, and if you try to run I'll turn the machine on you and use its destroying rays. I must find out what my masters want.'

He let go of Spiky, pointed the machine heavenwards and began pressing the sides of it. The watchers saw rays shooting upwards, and then in return green rays flickered down from one of the bubbles. The tramp became excited, and began signalling back frantically. Suddenly rays of a purple colour homed in on his head. With a cry he dropped his own ray machine, put his hands to his head and staggered around in the middle of the hollow. Spiky stood there as if numb, staring at him.

'Take the children into the woods!' the Chief of Police ordered Mr Browser.

'But what about Spiky?' demanded Anna.

'He'll have to take his chance,' replied the Chief. 'The lives of all the townspeople could be at stake –'

'We can't leave him!' said Mr Browser.

'P.C. Nixon – fire!' shouted the Chief of Police.

Mr Browser, Anna and Selwyn began to run towards Spiky, P.C. Nixon fired, and more rays descended all over the hollow. When they fell they zipped from place to place on the ground like firecrackers, and gradually a few wisps of mist began to rise from the ground. The tramp made a despairing grab at Spiky, who managed to disentangle himself just as Anna and Selwyn reached him.

'Get away quickly!' called out Mr Springfield, who was lying on the ground with his arms and legs bound. 'You'll all be poisoned!'

'Spiky! Are you all right?' cried Anna. Spiky nodded, fighting for breath.

'I'm all right, but you must save Mr Springfield. Either they'll take him or he'll be left to die. The capsules are breaking, Mr Browser – the poison cloud is forming!'

'He's right!' said Mr Browser. 'I've a knife here –'

He took out his old penknife and sawed away at the thin rope around Mr Springfield's wrists until at last it broke. By then the mist was swirling around the children's faces.

'Get them out, Mr Browser!' cried the Warden. 'Leave the knife with me, or you'll all be killed. I can see one of the bubbles coming down – run, for your lives!'

'Hold your breath and run!' shouted Mr Browser, and pushed Spiky on his way.

The three children ran ahead of him, mouths

tightly closed and eyes beginning to itch as the poison cloud started to take effect. As they ran they heard shots being fired, and the Chief of Police, a handkerchief over his nose and mouth, came to meet them.

They came out of the mist when they reached the edge of the hollow, where Spiky, exhausted, sank down against a tree trunk. The Chief of Police took his handkerchief from his mouth.

'Thank goodness, the cloud is rising straight upwards,' he said, as they all took in gulps of fresh air.

'It won't do that for long,' Spiky warned him. 'Soon it will float over Chivvy Chase School – that's where it always goes. And by the time it reaches there, it will be much thicker!'

They turned and looked back into the mist, which was slowly rising, like the mist you see over the countryside, only a metre or so high, on a summer's day just after dawn.

The Chief of Police, fascinated and amazed by what he was seeing, suddenly sprang into action.

'Mr Browser and the children, you had better go back to the cars. I've sent for reinforcements, and P.C. Nixon is trying to bring down the objects we thought we saw. I have two men going into the hollow from the other side in the hope of releasing the Warden and capturing the other man. I only hope they've reached them before the mist makes it impossible. We must do all we can to deal with this, for the sake of the whole town and perhaps the country. It seems as though the Warden's fears were well founded!'

P.C. Nixon came running towards them from around the edge of the hollow.

'I think I hit one, sir,' he said. 'The thing just disappeared, as if a bubble had burst.'

'Keep shooting,' ordered his Chief. 'Let's shoot down as many as we can, then perhaps we can investigate them.'

'It's getting difficult,' commented the marksman. 'The mist is hiding their movements.'

Mr Browser and the children, partly out of curiosity and partly because they knew they couldn't drive away in a police car without a policeman being present, stood a little distance away and watched and listened.

'Do you know what the tramp was up to?' Mr Browser asked Spiky.

'Until this happened, I thought he was mad,' admitted Spiky. 'He said he couldn't let me go because he was in the power of the Space Maggots, as he called them. Then he started signalling them, and I think they must have become angry with him, perhaps because we had found out about him, and he started signalling faster, and kept muttering, "No – no – no!" Then the rays started to come, and the cloud began to form, and he tried to get away, but he didn't want to leave me to escape –'

'We saw that,' said Mr Browser. 'Are you all right now, Simon?'

'I think so,' said Spiky. 'The cloud hadn't reached up to my face, but my eyes were already beginning to sting.'

'The cloud's going higher and higher,' said Anna.

The cloud, gathering strength, was a dense mass as it rose above the hollow, blacking out the sky and casting a gloomy shadow over the woods.

'If it does move over the school, we'd better give them a warning,' said Selwyn.

'The Chief of Police should be doing that,' said Mr Browser. 'Where has he gone?'

'Into the cloud, trying to find the tramp,' said Anna. 'Here he comes now.'

The Chief of Police had discovered that the cloud was no respecter of persons, and was as unpleasant to him as it had been to those under him.

'It's impossible to exist in that!' he declared. 'Our task now is to return to the cars and warn the town in case the cloud spreads that way.'

'You can see the whole of the hollow now,' called out Spiky. He was right. The grass in the hollow was visible again, most of it brown as though it had been burnt. Spiky looked curiously at the place where he had been held. Neither the Warden nor the tramp was anywhere to be seen, nor was the strange machine which the tramp had used. Only his half empty rucksack lay abandoned on the ground.

Cautiously the Chief of Police and one of his men walked to the middle of the hollow. The detective picked up the rucksack and looked inside it.

'Only a few old clothes in it,' he announced.

'Bring it with you,' ordered his Chief. 'Be quick – I don't like the look of that cloud. Who knows what

trouble it may cause if it descends on a crowded area.'

'Such as Chivvy Chase School,' shouted Mr Browser. 'Don't you believe what we've told you? Our school playing field isn't turning brown for no reason.'

'Then you'd better get back and warn them,' said the Chief of Police.

'Give us a driver, and we'll go,' called out Anna.

He gave her a sharp look, but realized that she was right, and ordered the detective to drive them back. A couple more policemen met them as they hurried along the path.

'Not a sign of either of them,' said one. 'They must have run away under cover of the cloud.'

'I don't believe it,' said Spiky. 'When I escaped from the tramp his eyes looked very strange, like those of hypnotized people.'

'Then what do you suggest has become of him?' asked the Chief a little sarcastically. 'Has he buried himself underground?'

'No – I think he may have been carried off by one of those bubble things, by the space creatures he talked about. Anything could have happened when the mist came up. I think they took his ray machine as well, so that we couldn't examine it. He said he was a kind of space agent. They left his rucksack behind because we couldn't learn anything from it.'

'Oh yes – and where are these space creatures supposed to have come from?'

'Through the hole in the ozone layer which has partly been made by our own pollution,' put in Mr Browser. 'We think they've taken over a disused satellite, which they are using as a kind of platform on their way to earth.'

The detective was so surprised that Mr Browser had answered him, and clearly taken his question seriously, that he said no more. The Chief of Police increased his pace. They passed the Warden's hut and went out of the Nature Reserve. Ten minutes later they were back in the cars, and radio messages were being passed all the time as they drove through the outskirts of the town.

The Chief of Police returned to the police station, but the detective first brought Mr Browser and the children back to Chivvy Chase School.

As Anna stepped out of the police car, she looked up at the sky.

'There's the cloud,' she said. 'It's hanging up there, high up and hardly moving.'

'Come quickly into school,' said Mr Bowser as the police car drove off.

They hurried up the path, and a strange feeling of unease filled the three children as they went. Chivvy Chase school was still and silent, like a deserted fortress.

'The door's locked, Mr Browser!' called out Spiky as he tried in vain to let himself into the school.

'Oh dear – I don't want to be caught in that cloud again!' wailed Anna.

Mr Browser banged on the door harder than anyone had ever done in the whole history of the school.

8 Sunshine Over Chivvy Chase

At first nothing happened in response to Mr Browser's knocking.

'Let us in!' called out Anna. 'If they don't, I'm going home,' she warned Mr Browser. Then they saw Miss Copewell's head appear round the door of the office. To Mr Sage's relief, she had come in late to school in spite of a splitting headache.

'Let us in!' called Mr Browser, pointing to the lock on the door. But Miss Copewell shook her head and walked out of their sight into the hall.

'They've had special instructions,' said Spiky. 'Are they afraid to let us in?'

'Perhaps they think we're poisonous,' suggested Selwyn.

'I'm going home,' threatened Anna, but at that moment Mr Sage appeared, with Miss Copewell behind him. Swiftly he opened the door and beckoned them inside. He looked hard and long at Spiky.

'So – you're back!' he said. 'And what have you been up to, Simon? You've caused a number of people a great deal of worry, my lad.'

Spiky looked to Mr Browser for assistance.

'He couldn't help it,' said Mr Browser. 'He was being held by a tramp in the woods, and he was lucky to escape with us.'

'Indeed?' said the Headmaster, and looked outside at the sun shining on the playground. 'I see no sign of any clouds,' he added. The longer life goes on in a normal way, the harder it is to believe that unusual happenings could occur, and Mr Sage was beginning to regret locking the doors of his school. He regretted it even more when a face appeared at the door and Mr Jolyon Morton, the Inspector, or Adviser, started pulling at it in order to enter.

'You'd better go back to your classroom at once,' said Mr Sage. 'I'll have to try and explain to Mr Morton why the door of the school is locked. He might think that we didn't want him to come in. I've set some work for Class 8, Mr Browser – you'd better mark it, because I shan't be able to come back to the classroom now that Mr Morton is here.'

'But the cloud is coming, Mr Sage. We saw it rising,' said Anna as Mr Sage moved to the door. 'And we saw some space things in bubble-like balloons, and they probably took the tramp away, and Mr Springfield too. They might have taken Spiky if he hadn't escaped!'

Mr Sage gave her a sideways look as he unlocked the door.

'The class have been working on some sums I put on the board,' he said. 'You'd better go and do some of them, Anna. You've wasted enough time as it is.'

Anna was upset but Mr Browser knew Mr Sage too well to allow her to go on trying to argue with him at such a time.

'Come along, you three,' he said. 'Mr Sage is quite right – we've been away from the classroom quite long enough.'

They moved away as Mr Jolyon Morton entered, but as the door opened the siren of a police car was to be heard in the background.

'Good morning, Mr Sage,' said the Inspector suspiciously. 'I thought for a moment that the school was closed because of a strike, or something. I didn't see a sign of life outside. It seems strange that no one is taking advantage of the fine weather to be out on the field or the playground today.'

'Do come in, and I'll try and explain,' said Mr Sage, wondering whether he dare tell Mr Morton why he had ordered the closing of all the doors and windows.

'We received a warning from the police,' he began, 'that there was likely to be a cloud of pollution passing over the school at some time this morning, and that all doors and windows should be closed.'

'Indeed?' said Mr Morton, raising his eyebrows – a movement he had practised to perfection. 'As far as I could tell, the sun was shining when I came in, and there wasn't much sign of clouds.'

'So far no,' agreed Mr Sage unhappily. 'But I can assure you the police were most concerned. They even took two of my children and a teacher out into the woods to find where the cloud was, and to try and locate a missing boy.'

Mr Morton looked at the Headmaster, and clearly was wondering whether poor Mr Sage was about to have a nervous breakdown.

'May I make you a cup of tea?' suggested the confused Headmaster.

'Ah, yes,' said the Inspector. 'I won't stay long, though. I just brought some papers for you to see.'

When Mr Sage left the room the Inspector stood by the window and decided that perhaps Mr Sage was under a strain of some kind; maybe the dinner money wouldn't come out right.

And then, quite suddenly, the sky turned dark and the sun disappeared, and Mr Morton saw a car moving slowly along the road outside the school. Someone was calling out a message from a loudspeaker fitted on top of the car. Mr Morton moved to the window to open it in order to hear what the message was, but before he could do so Mr Sage came rushing in and pulled him away from the window.

Mr Jolyon Morton was shocked. No one had laid hands on him since he was a boy at school.

'It's the cloud!' cried Mr Sage. 'We must keep all the doors and windows closed. The cloud has come!'

'Really!' said the Inspector, pulling his jacket into place again. 'You seem to be in a highly nervous state this morning. In view of what has happened, I shall leave at once. Here are the papers I brought you – if you wish to discuss anything, you can do so over the telephone, when you've calmed down. Goodbye, Mr Sage.'

He stalked out of the room wearing an expression of surprise and anger, while Mr Sage was left to fear that Chivvy Chase School would have to work very hard in future to come back into favour with Mr Jolyon Morton.

The Inspector opened the door, which Mr Sage had left unlocked, and walked out into the rainstorm which had just begun. Upstairs, Mr Sage's sums had lost their interest for Class 8, all of whom were at the windows looking out at the swirling, grey cloud which was wrapping itself around the school. Mr Browser was at the window too, for he was as curious as Spiky, Anna and Selwyn were to know what the cloud might bring. The rest of the class simply used the cloud as an excuse to break off from their work, especially as their teacher seemed to have lost interest in the sums too.

'It's nearly playtime,' said Michael Fairlie. 'It looks as if there'll be no play again today.'

'See that man going out into the rain?' called out Anna.

They could see the Inspector walking down the path by the side of the school. He had started off normally, then bent his head as if to protect himself against the wind, then put his hands to his eyes and began to stagger.

'He'll have to come back,' said Spiky, 'or he'll be blinded by the rain. It comes from the capsules – someone must warn him!'

To Mr Browser's surprise Spiky darted across the room and out of the door.

'I hope he's not going outside too,' said Mr Browser. 'I should have thought he'd had enough for one day!'

'Mr Browser! There's one of those bubble things!'

Anna was pointing out of the window, and as Mr Browser looked at the surging, swirling puffs of cloud, he thought for one second that she could be right.

'They're after Spiky, Mr Browser, because of all he knows about them – and I reckon they'll take him if he goes outside! Maybe he's still under their influence –'

'There he goes!' cried Selwyn. 'Come back, Spiky!'

Spiky couldn't hear him, of course, and he ran on towards the Inspector, who was now making no progress at all and looked about to fall flat on the ground.

'We must get them back!' cried Selwyn.

'I'm not going out there,' said Anna. 'I'm too scared!'

When he saw Spiky Jackson trying to pull the Inspector to his feet, Mr Browser decided that it was all or nothing now.

'Stay here!' he ordered Selwyn and the rest of the class. 'I must bring those two back!'

But as he went out of the door Selwyn turned to the others.

'We must help them,' he called out. 'Together perhaps we can surround them until they're back inside. Follow me!'

The rest of the class were so surprised to hear the

quiet Selwyn suddenly giving orders and disobeying Mr Browser that they decided something unusual must be happening, and hurried out of the classroom after him. Even Anna came fearfully after them. They flowed along the corridor and down the stairs like water from a burst pipe, and caught up Mr Browser just as he reached the front door.

'No running!' ordered Mr Sage, outraged at the sight. 'Mr Browser, stop them from running. And you can't go outside. Whatever do you think you're doing?'

His plea was unanswered as the wave of children surged past him.

They found Spiky struggling to help Mr Jolyon Morton to his feet, in the thickest part of the cloud, which had descended upon the school like a fog. Anna stood in the doorway as Mr Browser and his class rushed out to help.

'Make a circle round them!' she shouted. 'Don't let anyone get through!'

Mr Browser pulled the Inspector to his feet, and directed him and Spiky back towards the door.

'Lips closed!' he told them. 'Try not to breathe. Keep hold of me, Spiky, and I'll guide you back.'

'This rain tastes awful!' mumbled the Inspector.

'Lips closed!' repeated Mr Browser. They stumbled in the direction of the door, with the children all around them, except for Anna, who was still acting as a watchdog.

'They're coming!' she cried out suddenly. 'I can

hear that whirring sound – Spiky, they're after you! Hurry up, all of you.'

Mr Browser admitted afterwards that although he could have heard a whirring sound, when he tried to look upwards all he could see was thick cloud; but then he was concentrating on shepherding the Inspector and the children in through the front door. At last they were all inside, coughing and gasping, and many of them with tears rolling down their cheeks. Mr Browser came in too, and closed the door behind him. They all sat in the corridor, trying to recover themselves, with Mr Sage looking at them in amazement. They had broken his rules not once but several times, and deserved a telling off, but they all looked so distressed, including the Inspector, that he was more concerned with helping them to recover.

Gradually their breathing became normal, their eyes stopped streaming and the coughing died away. Like most Inspectors, Mr Morton could face the truth when danger threatened.

'My word, Mr Sage, you were right about that cloud,' he said. 'I've never been out in anything so poisonous. I don't know if I would have made it back to the school without the help of these children. I certainly wouldn't have reached my car. I'd like to thank you, Mr – er –'

'Browser,' said Mr Browser. 'But you mostly need to thank these children.' He pushed Spiky and Anna in front of the Inspector. 'Sometimes children seem to know more than they're given credit for,' he added.

'They were the first to realize the danger – apart from poor Mr Springfield.'

'Indeed, indeed, I'm sure I'm grateful to them,' said Mr Morton. 'But where does this poison cloud come from, Mr Sage?'

Mr Browser frowned, and Spiky was angry that the Inspector had chosen to ask the person least likely to know.

'I'm sure we'd all like to know,' replied Mr Sage.

'It comes from –' began Spiky – but Mr Sage silenced him with a look.

'There must be some factory giving off poisonous fumes,' decided the Inspector. 'There should be an inquiry about this.'

'No doubt there will be,' said Mr Sage.

'The sky's becoming brighter,' said Anna, and indeed the cloud was dispersing, rising upwards and spreading outwards very quickly.

'You'd better all go back to your classroom,' said Mr Sage.

'May we have playtime outside if the sun starts to shine?' asked Michael Fairlie.

'Perhaps,' replied the Headmaster. 'We shall have to check on the state of the ground first of all.'

Class 8 returned to their room, Mr Jolyon Morton drank a cup of tea with Mr Sage, having found that his time was not as short after all, and soon the sun began to shine and dried up the stains of the raindrops on the playground. Although the grass on the field looked browner than ever, the cloud had disappeared completely, leaving behind it no visible bad effects. At the same time as Anna Cardwell was pleading with Mr Browser that there was no good reason for playtime to be cancelled, Mr Sage went outside to make sure that it would be safe to ring the bell.

At the same moment Anna, looking out from the classroom window, and Mr Sage, looking across the playground to the school field, saw the figure of a man half lying, half sitting on the far side of the field. To Mr Sage it was the figure of an unknown man, and he wasted no time but ran in and phoned the police. He had suffered enough unusual happenings that morning, and he was taking no chances. To Anna, it was obvious who the man was.

'There's that tramp, Mr Browser! The one we saw in the woods. I bet he's been dropped out of one of those bubble things. Perhaps when they couldn't get Spiky, the Space Maggots decided to drop him!'

Spiky, like Mr Sage, had endured enough.

'Oh, shut up, Anna!' he said rudely – but he moved across to the window to take a good look. 'He seems half dead,' was his verdict.

'Go down and warn Mr Sage that there's a man on the field, Anna,' said Mr Browser. But by the time she was at the foot of the stairs Mr Sage had already rung the police, and they were on their way.

So once again playtime had to be delayed – this time because Mr Sage was waiting for the police to come and collect the man on the field. A police car and an ambulance arrived quickly, and the man was transferred to a stretcher. The detective who had been with them on the search for Spiky was there, and Mr Browser left his class in order to go out with Mr Sage and identify the man.

'He's definitely the man we saw in the woods,' declared Mr Browser, looking down at the tramp, who was now lying out flat on the stretcher, unconscious.

From an upper window Spiky, Anna and Selwyn were watching too, unknown to Mr Sage. The tramp had a gingery beard and straggly hair, and looked unshaven and dirty.

'That's him,' said Spiky. 'We ought to go down and find out what happened to him.'

'I saw him in that bubble,' insisted Anna. 'I bet they tipped him out when they found that too many people knew about them.'

'We should tell the police that,' said Selwyn.

'Maybe Mr Browser is doing that,' suggested Spiky hopefully.

But Mr Browser was having great difficulty in getting anyone to listen to him.

'That man could tell us about the capsules and what's happened to Mr Springfield,' he said.

'I doubt it,' said the detective impatiently. 'He's out cold now, and besides, we know about the cloud.'

'Know about it?' Mr Browser said, looking surprised and put out, because he believed he had earned the right to know about it too.

'Yes,' went on the detective, 'we understand from

our investigations that it was probably caused by a leak from a chemical factory some miles away.'

'Probably?' was all Mr Browser said, but his expression of disbelief said more.

'Well, according to what I've heard from very high up people, I could really say almost certainly,' declared the detective. 'After all, what else could have caused it?'

'What about the capsules?'

'Ah yes, those capsules. The Chief of Police himself has just told me that the capsules were really large dewdrops which were swollen by a chemical addition, probably because the leak from the chemical factory had been going on for some time.'

'But – the letter Mr Springfield wrote?'

'The fact that Mr Springfield has disappeared again backs up our idea that poor Mr Springfield has been unwell for some time.'

'But – the tramp had some sort of ray gun –'

The detective looked at Mr Browser with some pity, and Mr Browser felt desperate. It's difficult to argue with authority, as the children in his class could have told him.

'We saw no ray gun,' said the detective, 'and there is certainly no trace of one. This poor tramp seems to have been under the influence of drugs. Now I must leave you, Mr Browser. I hope you and your class will be able to get down to work again and forget all about this unfortunate affair. Goodbye.'

The tramp was being lifted into the ambulance,

and the engine of the police car started up. Mr Browser stood and watched both vehicles being driven away. His forehead was wrinkled because his mind was confused. He had many more questions which he would have liked to put to the detective, but deep down he knew they would all have been answered as smoothly and unsatisfactorily as the others. There was no one to back him up about the capsules and the ray machine, except for Anna and Spiky and Selwyn, and their word, he realized, would count for little because they were children. Even Mr Benchley of the Comprehensive School would not be believed against the word of experts in London.

'Well, George,' said Mr Sage, appearing suddenly at his side, 'that's all been cleared up neatly, hasn't it! The Chief of Police has been on the phone to me, and he explained it all. No doubt they'll make sure no more leaks occur at that factory –'

'Which factory?' asked Mr Browser bluntly. 'Did he name the factory?'

'No, no. It's a factory some miles from here,' said Mr Sage. 'By the way, as the playground is dry, and we've missed some playtimes lately, I'm going to ring the bell and allow the children out for a long playtime.'

'But – all this can't be true!' protested Mr Browser. 'I don't believe in the factory story, even if they name a factory, and I do believe the capsules came from –' he hesitated, and then came out with it – 'from the hole in the sky!'

'From where?' asked Mr Sage, looking sharply at Mr Browser.

'Never mind,' said Mr Browser sadly. 'I'll go and see that Class 8 are ready to come down when the bell rings.'

'That's more like it,' remarked Mr Sage. 'And kindly make sure that all of them go out, will you. I don't want any of them hanging back.'

When Mr Browser reached his classroom, Anna and Spiky and Selwyn were waiting for him.

'What's happened, Mr Browser?'

'Did the tramp tell them about the bubble thing?'

'Are they going to chase the Space Maggots?'

Mr Browser shook his head, and hadn't the heart to tell them that nobody believed what they thought had happened.

'It's time to go out to play,' he said. 'You must try and forget all about it. The sun is shining, so make the most of it. Class 8, stand! Lead on!'

Spiky, Selwyn and Anna tried to hang back.

'All of you!' ordered Mr Browser. 'At once!'

He looked so fierce that they had to obey him. When they had gone he sat down at his desk and remained quite still, staring out of the window at the sunshine. Could it all have happened as he had first thought, or was the cloud of pollution man-made? Was an attempted invasion of the earth by the Space Maggots under way? Whichever of these was true, would pollution win?

'Aren't you coming for a cup of tea, Mr Browser?'

asked Miss Causewell, the teacher from next door. 'Better make the most of a sunny playtime,' she added.

'There'll be more of those from now on, for a while,' said Mr Browser, and she wondered for a moment why he seemed so sure. But the real world is always with us, and we love to be swallowed up by it – and Mr Browser, in spite of his doubts, was no different from the rest. 'Summer's on its way at last,' he said, and walked with her along the corridor and down the stairs to the Staffroom.

Out in the playground, doubts were dying harder.

'I'm sure that tramp had a ray gun,' insisted Spiky, 'and I saw those maggot things up in the sky.'

'So did I,' said Selwyn.

'Maybe the tramp will tell the truth when he comes round,' said Anna hopefully. She was beginning to be more interested in skipping than in the morning's adventure. Spiky was drawn into a chasing game, and Selwyn was left to wander alone and try and puzzle out the mystery. And it was Selwyn who first saw a familiar figure coming up the path from the school gate.

'Spiky! Anna!' he shouted. 'Look who's coming!'

They looked up, and saw Mr Springfield walking towards the school gate. Anna dropped her skipping rope, and all three hurried from the playground to meet him.

'Mr Springfield! You're safe!' called out Selwyn.

'Yes, I've been home to tell your mother,' answered the Warden, 'and now I've come to thank Mr Browser and you children for helping to save me from that tramp.'

'And from the Space Maggots?' called out Spiky.

'And from the Space Maggots,' replied the Warden, smiling. 'But whether we're saved from them yet, who can say? They may be making use of that hole in the sky again, if we aren't careful. Where is Mr Browser?'

'In the Staffroom,' said Anna. 'But –'

But Mr Springfield waved them goodbye and walked into the school, leaving them to carry on with their games. The tramp never told his story, because as soon as he was better he disappeared. The grass on the school field began to grow green again, and the people of Chivvy Chase were assured that there would be no more leaks to endanger the area.

Yet when we hear of dying forests and poisoned rivers and chemical leaks can we be sure that all this is being caused only by man? Or are the enemies from space continuing to build up their attacks on Earth? Surely human beings wouldn't want to destroy themselves?

The trouble is that Mr Browser, like the rest of the grown-ups, is too busy working to give much thought to it; and the children, like Anna and Spiky and Selwyn, are too busy playing to bother about such things.

Long may the sun shine on Chivvy Chase School –
but beware of the space capsules. One day they may
be back.

Some other Puffins

THE SILK AND THE SKIN
Rodie Sudbery

What are Ralph and his gang always doing in the church-yard? Guy just *has* to find out, although it's obvious they're up to no good. He soon discovers that he and his backward younger brother are being drawn into a nightmarish situation – but where is Guy going to find the courage to stand up against Ralph and his gang – and the forces of the super-natural they've already summoned . . .?

SUMMER FOR A LIFETIME
Brigid Chard

Dan feels a failure – and when he is sent to his uncle's farm to recover from an operation, his confidence is at its lowest ebb. But soon not getting into his brother's school ceases to seem so important as Dan's priorities change and his life finds a new direction. Who could have guessed at the thrill of snaring a rabbit, seeing a calf born, or training your very own ferret? Under the expert guidance of wily old ex-gamekeeper Ben Hugget, Dan develops skills he never dreamt he had and gradually learns a new self-respect.

THE MINERVA PROGRAM
Claire Mackay

Here at last is Minerva's chance to be out in front, to be really good at something – computers. That's where her future lies. But that future is threatened when Minerva is almost too clever for her own good. Suddenly she is accused of cheating and is banned from the computer room. It takes the combined talents of 'Spiderman', her brother, and her inventive friends to solve this intriguing mystery.

ROSCOE'S LEAP
Gillian Cross

To Hannah, living in a weird and fantastical old house means endlessly having to fix things like heating systems and furnaces, but for Stephen it is a place where something once happened to him, something dark and terrifying which he doesn't want to remember but cannot quite forget. Then a stranger intrudes upon the family and asks questions about the past that force Hannah to turn her attention from mechanical things to human feelings, and drive Stephen to meet the terror that is locked away inside him, waiting . . .

OVER THE MOON AND FAR AWAY
Margaret Nash

The new girl at school calls herself a 'traveller' and says she comes from beyond the stars. Ben doesn't believe her, of course, but then again Zillah isn't quite like anyone he and his friends have ever met. There's her name for a start, and she doesn't even know how to play their games. But the mysterious newcomer does seem able to make things happen . . .

THE TROUBLE WITH JACOB
Eloise McGraw

Right from the start there is something very weird about the boy Andy sees on the hillside. Every time Andy's twin sister Kat is there he just disappears, and all he ever talks about is his bed! Andy thinks he's going mad, but then he and Kat decide that someone is playing tricks on them. There must be some logical solution to the mystery. After all, the only other explanation would be far too incredible . . .

THE BURNING QUESTIONS OF
BINGO BROWN
Betsy Byars

Has there ever been a successful writer named Bingo? Has there ever been a successful person with freckles? These are just some of the burning questions in Bingo Brown's life – but where is he going to find the answers? When his worst enemy moves in next door and Bingo keeps falling in love, he knows the question marks are getting larger. But with The Most Thrilling Day and The Worst News of his life still to come, Bingo finds he has a long way to go!

PRINCESS FLORIZELLA
Philippa Gregory

Poor Princess Florizella! She really isn't like other princesses at all. She isn't beautiful. She wants to share her palace with people who don't have homes. She loves eating huge meals, and she refuses to be rescued by a handsome prince, and never wants to marry anyone. But unfortunately her parents, a very ordinary King and Queen, have other ideas in mind.

MAGGIE AND ME
Ted Staunton

Maggie is the undisputed Greenapple Street Genius. She's always got some brilliant plan – and Cyril inevitably has to help her. Whether it's getting back at the school bully or swapping places for piano lessons, these best friends are forever having adventures. Poor Cyril! Life without Maggie would be an awful lot easier, but then it would be much more boring. What would he do if she ever moved away? Ten stories about the intrepid duo.

THE BEWITCHING OF ALISON ALLBRIGHT
Alan Davidson

Alison has always sought refuge in day-dreams: of a lovely home, of being an exciting person, of doing all that the others at school do – and more. Dreams ... until Mrs Considine appears, spinning her amazing web of fantasy, creating another life for Alison out of those dreams. There is no magic in the bewitching of Alison Allbright, only the hypnotically dazzling lure of that other life. Until it's clear enough to see clearly.

STAN
Ann Pilling

Stan couldn't have been more unlucky in running away from his London foster home, for he gets unwittingly caught up in the activities of vicious criminals and is pursued by one of them who will stop at nothing to get what he wants. But throughout his terrifying journey to Warrington and Liverpool and across the Irish Sea, Stan never loses hope of the determination to find his brother and the home he dreams of.

DREAM HOUSE
Jan Mark

For Hannah, West Stenning Manor is a place of day-dreams, but for Dina its attraction lies in the celebrities who tutor the courses there. But when a well-known actor arrives, hotly pursued by his attention-seeking daughter, Julia, Dina begins to realize that famous people are no better than ordinary ones. A warm and tremendously funny story by the author of *Thunder and Lightnings*.

MIRACLE AT CLEMENT'S POND
Patricia Pendergraft

When Lyon and his friends find a baby abandoned by Clement's Pond it seems common sense to leave it on the doorstep of the poor old village spinster, Adeline, who has longed for a baby all her life. All the children think it's the perfect answer to the problem at the time, but as Lyon is to find out, there are unforeseen complications to follow.

LAURIE LOVED ME BEST
Robin Klein

Julia hates the hippie-like commune where her mother has taken them both to live. And Andre feels stifled by her father's rigid ways. Together they seek refuge in an abandoned cottage behind their school and begin to make it their ideal home. However, their private lives amazingly remain a mystery to each other, so when a gorgeous 18-year-old boy turns up, they're soon unwittingly competing for his charms.

LIONEL THE LONE WOLF
Linda Allen

While travelling by train to visit his Uncle Richard, Lionel overhears two men plotting a murder – or so he thinks. The worst part of it is, his uncle is their target! Being a fast-thinking private investigator isn't as easy as Lionel had imagined. But then he suddenly has a brilliant idea and, with the help of his uncle, 'the lone wolf' cracks the mystery.